AFTER
THE
GAME

Also by Abbi Glines

The Field Party Series
Until Friday Night
Under the Lights

AFTER THE GAME

Abbi Glines

SIMON & SCHUSTER

First published in Great Britain in 2017 by Simon and Schuster UK Ltd
A CBS COMPANY

First published in the USA in 2017 by Simon Pulse,
an imprint of Simon & Schuster, Inc.

1 3 5 7 9 10 8 6 4 2

Simon & Schuster UK Ltd
1st Floor
222 Gray's Inn Road
London WC1X 8HB

Simon & Schuster Australia, Sydney
Simon & Schuster India, New Delhi

A CIP catalogue record for this book
is available from the British Library.

ISBN: 978-1-4711-2506-5
Ebook ISBN: 978-1-4711-2507-2

Printed and bound by CPI Group (UK) Ltd, Croydon, CR0 4YY

www.simonandschuster.co.uk
www.simonandschuster.com.au
www.simonandschuster.co.in

MIX
Paper from
responsible sources
FSC® C020471

Simon & Schuster UK Ltd are committed to sourcing paper
that is made from wood grown in sustainable forests and support the Forest
Stewardship Council, the leading international forest certification organisation.
Our books displaying the FSC logo are printed on FSC certified paper.

For every teenage girl who has made a mistake and those who had no one to believe in them. May you find strength in yourself and realize you are strong enough. This too shall pass, and you'll become a woman of strength. Hang in there.

I'm Some Hungwy

CHAPTER 1

RILEY

The crash from the kitchen jerked me out of my dreams and into reality. Something was burning and Bryony wasn't in bed beside me. Her sweet blond curls and big blue eyes were what normally met me when I opened my eyes.

Jumping up, I ran through the already open door of my bedroom and sprinted toward the kitchen. A million things ran through my mind as I went the short distance. Bryony never got out of bed without me. Another crash happened just as I turned the corner into the kitchen.

My grandmamma was standing at the sink with a frantic look on her face. The pot on the floor had been full of uncooked oats and milk, which were now splattered on the tile floor. Smoke was coming from the toaster behind her, and I moved quickly to jerk the plug out of the wall before things got worse.

"Momma," Bryony's sweet voice called out from behind me.

Spinning around, needing to see her face and know she was okay, I almost slipped on the milk under my feet.

The wild curls of her hair were sticking up everywhere as she stared up at me with wide eyes and a frown. "I'm some hungwy," she said.

I reached down to pick her up before she stepped into the mess on the floor and cradled her against me. Holding her was enough reassurance to calm me down.

"Grandmamma was trying to fix you something, I see," I said, looking toward my grandmother, who was now looking down at the spilled breakfast at her feet.

"I don't know," Grandmamma said. Her voice sounded lost, like she wasn't sure what she was saying or why she was standing there. This was normal for her. Some days were better. Others were not. Today was not going to be a good day.

"I'll put Bryony in her high chair and get her some cereal, and then I'll clean this up. What do you want me to fix you, Grandmamma?" I asked her.

She turned her gaze to mine, and the confusion there always made me sad. The woman who had taught me to make biscuits and sang me songs while playing the pots and pans like drums was no longer there. She was lost inside her head.

"I don't know," she said, which were words I heard often.

I moved over to put Bryony in her high chair before going to take my grandmamma's arm and move her away from the slippery mess. Most mornings I woke up earlier than my grandmother. Today I had overslept. My mom normally woke me up before she left for work, but today she either had tried and failed or had forgotten.

"I'm some hungwy," Bryony said again. That was her way of telling me she wanted food, and now. If she'd woken up and found Grandmamma in the kitchen, she would have told her the same thing. For a moment, Grandmamma had known that meant she needed to feed her. But that brief memory left and she had dropped a pot. A dish was also broken on the floor with what looked like applesauce on it. Then, of course, the burned toast.

"Okay," I told her and reached for a box of cereal to place some on her tray. "Eat this and let Mommy clean up the mess."

Bryony picked up a piece of the round oat cereal and put it in her mouth.

"I broke a plate." Grandmamma's voice was full of concern.

"It's okay. Accidents happen. I'm going to clean this up, then I'll make you some of your favorite steel-cut oats with brown sugar and apple slices. Okay?" I assured her with a smile.

She frowned. "That's my favorite?"

It was like dealing with another child. We hadn't been back in Lawton, Alabama, long, but the time we had been back hadn't been easy. Watching someone you love so much live lost in their own head was heartbreaking. Alzheimer's was a terrible disease.

"Gandma hungwry," Bryony told me.

I turned my attention to my daughter and smiled. "Yes, she is. It's breakfast time."

"Sandra will be upset about her plate. She loved those plates. I'll need to go into town and buy her a new one at Miller's. Least I can do."

To anyone else, those words might have sounded sane. Logical. But they were anything but. For starters, Sandra was my grandmamma's sister who had passed away from cancer when I was three years old. And Miller's hadn't been open for business since 1985. The only reason I knew this was because Grandmamma had sent me to fetch something at Miller's when we first moved back and I'd started out the door when Momma stopped me and explained. Grandmamma was living in the past. Roy Miller had passed away of a heart attack in '85, and his family had closed the store and moved out of Lawton.

Instead of reminding her of all this, though, I had found

just going along with it was easier. If I told her Sandra was dead or that Miller's was closed, she'd go into a fit of hysteria. That was what she knew and remembered today. So I ignored her comment and cleaned up the floor before getting a pot of oats on the stove cooking properly, then disposed of the burned toast out the back door.

"Do you know where I put Lyla's applesauce? She needs to eat some this morning. I made it fresh yesterday from the apples I got at Miller's."

Lyla was my mother. That was another thing that Grandmamma confused. She often thought Bryony was my mother when she was a baby. Again lost in the past.

"I'll get her some applesauce. You just sit there and relax. I'll get you some juice. Watch the pretty birds outside. They're eating the birdseed we put out yesterday." That got her attention, and she began watching out the large bay window for the birds.

Mom only worked until noon today at the hospital. I would be able to take Bryony out for a walk and to the park after lunch. I needed to get them fed and start the morning chores so we would have plenty of time later to go play. The sun was shining and the warm days were behind us. The cool autumn air was perfect for being outside. And Bryony loved to pick up the different-colored leaves on the ground. She called them her "cowection."

*Don't Let Your Good-Guy
Complex Make You Crack*

CHAPTER 2

BRADY

Week two of life without Ivy, and the drama was still going strong. I had thought finally cutting her free would make both of us happier, especially me. But Ivy crying in the halls and leaving me sad texts about being lost without me wasn't easier. I didn't like knowing I'd hurt her. But I couldn't help it. It was either end it or continue letting her pretend we were something we weren't.

Truth was, if I had really loved her I wouldn't have wanted another girl. I may not have gotten the other girl, but I'd wanted her. That right there was me not treating Ivy right. Breaking up with her had been the fair thing to do. But to watch her carry on, you'd think otherwise.

"Be strong. Don't let your good-guy complex make you crack," West Ashby said as he walked up beside me in the hallway. He was one of my best friends. Possibly my only best friend. Since I may have been in love with my other best friend's girlfriend at some point. I wasn't sure about that, really.

"She's not taking this well," I replied, refusing to look toward Ivy and her group of friends, who were all watching me. I could feel every eye on me like hot daggers. I wasn't the guy who got angry glares. That was the sort of thing West or Gunner would get. Not me. I was the good guy.

"It was time. You'd suffered long enough for the sake of being nice. Sometimes you need to learn to say *fuck this* and move on."

"I don't want your reputation," I said, cutting my eyes at him.

He chuckled as if that was amusing. "My reputation is that of a man in love. All my previous transgressions have been washed away."

He was right. My cousin Maggie had changed him. He no longer used girls and tossed them away. Seeing him with Maggie made me want that too. A girl who I wanted to be near. A girl who made me smile just at the sight of her. A girl like Willa, who was now with Gunner, and I didn't stand a chance. Nor would I even try because they were happy together. I had never really seen Gunner happy before. Willa seemed to make him that way.

"Ivy isn't *it*, you know? She deserves to be that girl for some guy. I'm just not that guy. Getting her to see that, however, seems impossible."

"Ivy is the purest case of clingy there is," West said, then slapped me on the back. "This is my stop. Be tough. She'll move on eventually."

I felt like that was my fault too. The way people looked at Ivy as a desperate girl unable to let go. I had let her hang on so long she had become just that, and it was all on me. If I had been fair months ago, this wouldn't be an issue. But I had made the situation worse by letting her still believe there was an *us*.

Gunner's laughter caught my attention, and I turned to see him with his arm around Willa's shoulder, smiling down at her like she was his only source of sunshine. I should be happy for them. But I wasn't. I wanted that. I had thought Willa would be that for me. Again, though, my fault. I hadn't really made a move with Willa and had let go of Ivy. Had I expected Willa to just hang around while I figured out what to do with my girlfriend? Apparently. I was a dumbass.

Willa turned her gaze and it met mine. She smiled. Not the flirty smile I got from most girls, but a friendly one.

The kind that a girl gives a guy when she sees him as a friend and wants nothing more.

I retuned the smile and nodded to Gunner before ducking into my next class and away from their lovefest. I wasn't a bitter person before now. But seeing them together was getting to me. Daily. It was the reason I had finally cut Ivy free. At least I had them to thank for that.

Asa Griffith and Nash Lee were sitting in their seats already. Both looked amused at something on Nash's laptop. I headed over to them and took a seat across from Nash and behind Asa.

"Hey, Brady," a blonde I'd seen before but had no idea what her name was said as I sat down. She did a fluttery finger wave.

"Go there for me," Asa said as he turned to see who was talking to me. "She's got a body. Test it out and tell me all about it."

I could tell from here she had a large chest size. That was all Asa was worried about. I looked at him and away from the girl. She wasn't the first female to suddenly start speaking to me. I'd been getting this all week. But I just couldn't do that to Ivy yet. She was still showing up with red, swollen eyes.

"More to a girl than her body," I told him under my breath.

He raised his eyebrows as if he were shocked. "Really?"

He was kidding, but it was still an asshole thing to say.

"Then you won't care about what Nash got in his e-mail this morning," Asa said, shooting a grin toward Nash.

I was afraid to ask.

"Hey, I didn't ask for it. She sent it on her own," he said in defense, as if he needed to justify whatever it was.

"But you're sure as hell gonna watch it over and over," Asa smirked.

Nash's dimples popped and he shrugged before closing his laptop and stowing it in his book bag. "I'm a guy and she's naked. Hell yes, I'm gonna watch it."

I didn't ask who it was because now I had a mental image playing in my head of what they were watching, and I didn't want a face to go with it.

"Y'all seen Riley around town? I saw her yesterday with some kid in a stroller. Like a little kid. She was leaving the park." Asa was frowning like he knew this wasn't good news, but he thought he should share it. We all didn't want to see Riley around. She was trouble. And Gunner was finally happy.

"Yeah, I saw her with the baby a couple weeks back. Her parents must have had another kid. Think she's getting homeschooled. Mom said her grandmother has Alzheimer's and her parents moved back to help take care of her." I had come home complaining about Riley being back in town, and Momma had straightened me out real quick.

"Sucks for the Lawtons. They've had enough shit this month. Riley showing back up ain't helping," Asa said.

"I ain't so sure I feel sorry for the Lawtons. Rich-people problems don't really compare to dealing with Alzheimer's," was Nash's response.

As much as I hated it for Gunner, I had to agree with Nash. They had their problems, but obviously so did Riley's family. Wasn't their fault that their daughter was a liar. I could hate her and also feel bad for her parents. They'd been through a lot too. But a new baby was a good thing. That had to have come just in time to help heal the mess Riley had made with her lies.

My Little Sister?

CHAPTER 3

RILEY

Rain. Seriously? It had been all sunshine when I had strolled Bryony to the park. The rainstorm came out of nowhere. And my mother wasn't answering her phone. It wasn't like she could leave Grandmamma at home to come get us anyway.

At least there was a cover on the stroller. I was going to get drenched when I moved out from under the minimal shade of this tree, but Bryony should stay somewhat covered.

"Wain, Momma!" she squealed, reaching her hands out to feel the drops. It didn't seem to be a bad thing for her. She liked it. This was an adventure. I tried to think of things like this as a new memory to make. Something to experience. It helped me deal with otherwise stressful moments. Before

Bryony, I didn't think that way. I got all upset over every-thing. Little things were a big deal. Like not being asked to prom by the guy you wanted or your best friend flirting with your boyfriend. Drama that seemed pointless to me now.

When she was placed in my arms, my world tilted. My life would never be the same, and all the pain that had led to her arrival in this world was gone. Just like that. I no longer cared about the past. I just cared that she was mine. Who her father was and what he had done meant nothing. Not now. Not ever.

I had my daughter. She was healthy. It became the only important thing in my life. Sleepless nights became a special time for us to bond. Endless crying when she didn't feel good became a chance to learn how to make her laugh. That was what mattered. The two of us.

"Yes, it's raining, baby girl. Let's see how fast we can get home," I said with a cheery tone.

She clapped in response, and I pulled my hoodie over my head to fight off the wetness for at least a few minutes before running toward the sidewalk that led to my grandmother's. It wasn't so bad. The fall air smelled good damp. It reminded me of my childhood. Those were good memories, ones I wanted for Bryony. Although we wouldn't be able to stay in Lawton. As much as I missed the town that had been part of me, it no longer accepted me. For now we would make our home here. Keep to ourselves and enjoy life. But it wasn't permanent.

A truck slowed beside me, and I kept jogging. I didn't turn to see who it was. I had a mission.

"You need a ride?" a familiar voice called out. I still didn't turn my head. I'd know Brady Higgens's voice anywhere. The hateful looks and words that I remembered from him kept my gaze straight and my feet moving.

"Jesus, Riley, it's pouring and the baby is getting all wet. At least get in for her sake. She's gonna get sick."

He sounded exasperated. I didn't like the tone of his voice or him thinking he should guide me in the way I was raising my child. A little rain wasn't going to make her sick. This wasn't the last frontier, for crying out loud.

"You've got another two miles to your grandmother's house. This storm is gonna get worse. Let me give you a ride. For the baby's sake."

The way he said *baby* infuriated me. He didn't realize who Bryony was. He along with all the other idiots in this town thought I'd lied. Accused me of it and ran me out of town. All because it wasn't possible that golden boy Rhett Lawton would rape me. I had to have come on to him. He had to have been the one to push me away. I was his brother's girlfriend, after all. Why would he rape me? I *must* be crazy.

I stopped running and turned to look at Brady. He had always been the good guy. Taking up for people and believing the best in them. Except for me. He'd turned on me just like the others had. I was about to open my mouth and tell him exactly where he could shove his almighty tone when the sky roared and lightning shot across the sky. Rain I wasn't scared of, but I didn't want Bryony out in an actual storm. My scathing words fell away and instead I said, "Okay."

He nodded, looking relieved I'd given in, and jumped out of the truck to grab the stroller after I lifted Bryony into my arms. "Just throw it in back. It's wet anyway. I'll have to set it out in the sun tomorrow to dry it."

I didn't wait to see if he did as I said. I hurried around to the passenger side and climbed in, with Bryony smiling as the raindrops pelted her face. The heat was on in the truck, and her little shiver made me worried Brady could be right and she might get a cold from this. I would get her some orange juice and a warm bath as soon as we got home.

Brady climbed back inside, and I grudgingly glanced at him and forced the words "Thank you" out of my mouth. Not something I'd ever expected to say to him or anyone around here.

He looked at Bryony. "I doubt your parents would want you walking your little sister home in this weather. I'm just glad you agreed to get in."

My little sister? Really? That was what they were saying

in town? I frowned and turned my attention toward the window to look out. I could correct him, but what good would that do? None. He would assume I got knocked up after I left town. Never could my actual story have been true. Although if one took the time to really see her, Bryony looked like a Lawton. She had many of her father's features. I wasn't going to point that out, though. I never wanted her to know the Lawtons. They were monsters.

My brother, Vance, had stayed when we left and dealt with all of this. He'd hated them all. But his life had been here. With me gone, the gossip died, and he was able to continue. The talk about my return, however, ended up getting him suspended twice for fighting. He agreed he'd rather go to the private school near where we had been living that had accepted him. He had backed out when we decided to return to be with my grandmother, but my parents believed that it was best for him to finish his school away from Lawton. His IQ was ridiculously high, but so was his temper. I felt guilty for putting him in this situation. When he left last week, he had told me that this was what he wanted to do and not to feel guilty. I'd cried anyway.

Bryony stuck her little chubby hands out toward the heat and turned to Brady to flash him her smile. She had no idea that he was an enemy. I didn't want her to know about enemies or ugliness in the world.

"What's her name?" he asked.

"Bryony," I replied. I didn't want to talk to him. He didn't want me in his truck any more than I wanted to be in it. Had it been any other of Gunner Lawton's friends that had driven by, I'd still be out in the storm, trying not to panic. Brady Higgens wasn't like that, though. He saw a baby in need, and he couldn't ignore it.

"You've got pretty eyes, Bryony," he told her.

She tilted her head back and looked up at me. Her damp blond curls stuck to her forehead. I bent my head and kissed that spot. It was hard not to.

"How old is she?"

Again I didn't want to chat with him, but he was giving us a ride. So if he wanted to pretend that he cared, I would try and participate. "Fifteen months."

"Wain!" she cheered as lightning struck outside.

Brady chuckled. She was adorable. He was going to be smitten before we got to my grandmother's.

"You're a big girl, then," he said to her.

She nodded her head vigorously. She liked being called big. Even though she also still liked for me to rock her to sleep at night and cuddle her like a baby.

"Does your grandmother still live in the same house?" he asked as he turned down her street.

"Yes." He would know how to get there. We'd grown

up together. Been at the same school, gone to the same parties, played at the same park.

Finally he pulled into her driveway, and I wrapped my arms tightly around Bryony. I needed to get her inside before I got the stroller.

"Let me run her inside, then I'll get the stroller," I told him.

"I got the stroller. Y'all go on in."

I didn't argue. Opening the truck door I hurried up the sidewalk to the safety of the house. Walking inside I called out for Mom, but she didn't answer. I wanted to hand her Bryony so I could run back out and get the stroller. Instead I set her down. "Wait right here. Let me get your stroller."

She nodded, and I turned to walk back out when Brady ran up to the door holding her saturated stroller.

"Thank you," I said again.

He nodded. "You're welcome."

Bryony's small hand tugged at my pants leg. "Momma is wet."

Brady's eyes widened, and I realized what she had just said. Guess he knew now. She wasn't my little sister after all.

I gave him a tight smile and closed the door before he could say anything else.

CHAPTER 4

BRADY

Momma? She'd called Riley Momma. I had heard it, and the look in Riley's eyes had confirmed it. Which meant what? Had she gotten pregnant that soon after leaving town?

Or before? Could her lie about Rhett been her way of trying to pin her pregnancy on someone she thought she could get money out of? If so, that was sucky. She'd almost ruined Rhett's future over her need to land someone as a father. It couldn't have been Gunner's because she hadn't slept with him. We all knew it. Someone had gotten in her pants, so she'd had to lie. That much was obvious.

Had she cared too much about Gunner to sleep with him? That was what I'd never understood. Why lie on his older brother? Why not lie on her boyfriend? Unless she thought Rhett was more believable than Gunner. I guessed I'd never understand why she did that. No point in trying to figure her out.

Fact was, Riley had a kid now and the little girl was cute. She appeared to be a good mom, but then I'd barely seen them together. She could be a terrible mom for all I knew.

The whole experience with Riley and Bryony stayed with me the rest of the evening. I didn't tell anyone I'd given her a ride simply because I didn't want to explain myself. I shouldn't have to. I'd like to think any of my friends would have done the same. She'd had a baby and it was storming. But I wasn't so sure. The hate they all had for her ran deep.

Although I had seen an ugly side to Rhett recently. He clearly wasn't above being an ass, especially to Gunner. I wondered if Gunner could believe Riley now that he knows the kind of person Rhett really is.

The idea that it was possible Riley hadn't been lying was there. But I just couldn't bring myself to accept that Rhett was so twisted and sick he'd actually rape her and lie about it. He had his issues, but he wasn't cruel. Not like that.

Shaking my head and wishing I could get all this out of it and think about something else, I headed for the attic stairs to escape to my bedroom, which was now up there.

My old bedroom door was open, and my cousin Maggie

was sitting on the bed with a book in her hand. I paused and stopped at the door.

"Where's West?"

She glanced up. "He's spending the afternoon with his mom."

He was good about that. Making sure his mother was okay and staying stable. After his father's death, they had been through some rough patches.

"That's good," I said, still standing there.

Maggie folded the page and closed the book in her lap. "You need to talk about something, Brady?" She tilted her head and studied me like she already knew the answer to this.

Maybe I did need to talk.

I shrugged. "Not sure."

She sighed and held up her book. "Might as well talk. You've interrupted my reading."

I knew if anyone would keep their mouth shut, it was Maggie. She didn't stir drama or participate in it. She also paid more attention to people than most, and I trusted her opinion.

I walked into the room and sat across from her in the chair that was placed in the corner.

"I gave Riley Young a ride home in the storm. She had a kid with her. A little girl not much older than a baby, really." There. I had admitted it.

Maggie stared at me a moment and said nothing. "Is that it? You gave a girl a ride and you feel the need to open up about it?"

I thought Maggie had heard the story of Riley Young already. "Did you miss the part where I said Riley Young? As in the girl who accused Rhett of rape and almost lost him his scholarship?"

"I know who Riley Young is. Y'all have bashed her enough. I'm aware of the story. But she had a small child with her, there was a storm, and she was out in it with the child. I would think anyone would offer her a ride. If you hadn't, then you should feel bad. But you did, so I'm not getting what this whole conversation is about."

Sighing, I leaned back in the chair and stared out the window a moment. How could I explain this to Maggie? She didn't jump on the team of hating anyone. She was patient and forgiving.

"The little girl called Riley *Momma*," I said, hoping to get more of a response from her.

Maggie's eyes widened. "Oh, so she has come back with a baby. Could it be Rhett's?"

Finally she was getting it. "That's what has me thinking. She lied on Rhett to get money out of him when she found out she was pregnant. That is all that makes sense. And when Gunner finds out about this, his life is going

22

to get even more complicated. He has enough on him as it is."

The frown on Maggie's face looked firmly directed at me. As if I had done something wrong. "Or Riley could have been telling the truth. From the little I saw of Rhett Lawton, I don't rank him high up there in moral standards. Why are you all so sure she lied?"

The same exact thing that had been plaguing me came so easily out of her mouth. But then, she wasn't talking about a guy who had been like an older brother to her. She didn't know Rhett. Not like I did.

"Rhett was a talented athlete. His family was the wealthiest in town. He was powerful, and the town made him feel that way. Is it so hard to believe he could take something that wasn't his? If he was everything all of you claim, then why did Riley try and pin it, as you say, on Rhett? Wouldn't she have known that it wasn't going to end well if she did? If it had been me I would have been terrified to lie on Rhett Lawton. Just seems she took a very scary route to make things easier on herself."

Everything she said made sense. All of it. But I couldn't just believe Riley or reach out to her. She was still the enemy. But what if she was innocent?

I stood up. "It's not that easy," was all I could say.

Maggie shrugged. "No, it's not. Especially for Riley."

CHAPTER 5

RILEY

No Lawton had shown up at my door to demand I leave
town. That was a good sign. It was possible Brady was
being the good guy that he liked to wear as his label and
keeping his mouth shut. The last thing I wanted was a
Lawton to show up and demand to see Bryony.

I wish I'd never told anyone the truth. If I had just
kept quiet about the father and left town quietly, then this
wouldn't be a problem. Bryony never needed to know who
her father was. I dreaded the day she'd ask me about him,
because I knew it was coming. When she started school and
realized the other kids had two parents, she was going to
want to know.

Right now she had my dad, and her pops was good enough. She wasn't lacking for attention and love. I was thankful for my parents and their support through all of this. Not once did they question my story. When everyone else had called me a liar, I had feared that they might too. But they hadn't.

Instead, they quit their jobs, found work far away from here, and moved us out of this town. All for me. I'd never forget that sacrifice. Because of them I had never felt alone through the process. Many girls weren't as lucky. I had met several at the teen pregnancy support group I went to once a week. I'd fought the idea at first when my mother brought home the pamphlet. But one day I decided it wouldn't hurt to give it a shot.

Those meetings gave me the courage to become a mother. They helped me realize I wasn't the only girl out there in this situation. They saved me in ways my parents couldn't. One day I intended to start my own facility for teen moms.

"Momma, samich." Bryony was tugging on my jeans asking for her favorite snack. Two pieces of toast with ketchup in the middle, cut up into four small squares, with no crust.

I bent down and pulled her close to me in a tight hug. "I love you," I told her.

"Okay," was her reply, followed by a wet kiss to my cheek.

I couldn't imagine my life without her. I didn't want to. The pain that Rhett put my family and me through was all worth it for this. My daughter. I'd live through it all again if I could have this.

"Where is Thomas?" Grandmamma asked, walking into the living room with a confused frown on her face. Thomas was the cat she had when I was a little girl, and he had passed away from cancer when I was nine.

"Around here somewhere," I replied. There was no use telling her he was dead. It would upset her, and she'd just start asking for him again in thirty minutes.

"I'm going to fix Bryony a snack. Come to the kitchen with us and I'll slice you up a pear with some cottage cheese."

She paused, still searching the room with her eyes for Thomas. "Do I like that?" she asked me.

Pears and cottage cheese had been her favorite snack for as long as I could remember. "You love it."

She nodded then sighed with a sag to her shoulders. She would start looking for Thomas again soon. But for now it seemed like she might be letting it go.

"Okay," she replied, and I took Bryony's hand and led them both toward the kitchen.

Mom was taking a nap. When Bryony and I got home from the park, she often went directly to bed for an hour. She needed it with her work schedule. Dad would get home from work at six, and she liked to be cooking dinner by the time he walked in the house.

"Let's turn on the television and see if one of your afternoon shows is on," I told Grandmamma. Mom had left Grandmamma's television in the kitchen. She said we needed to keep things as they were to avoid confusion. Mom had always been against having TVs in the house, but she kept this one around for Grandmamma.

"Okay," she agreed, still frowning.

Coming back here had been scary. My only other option had been to raise Bryony alone. I wasn't ready for that. Not yet. I was still homeschooling on the Internet to get through high school. I wanted to give Bryony a good life. One where I had a real job and could support us.

My parents had worried about me coming back too, but I understood their need to be with Grandmamma. After the call she had been found at three in the morning banging on the door of the grocery in town demanding bananas, we all knew there was no other option. None of us wanted to put her in a home.

Hiding indoors with Bryony wasn't fair to her either. She loved the park and playing outside. I had made the decision to face this town head on and whatever they said didn't matter. Small-minded people in a small town. This didn't affect my future.

However, saying that and believing it are two different things. It wasn't easy to see people from my past and be treated as if I were the plague. Those who were once friends now acted like I wasn't there or scowled at me.

All because I asked my boyfriend's older brother for a ride home from a field party after I had fought with Gunner. I had trusted Rhett. That was my only mistake. I had done nothing else wrong.

Holding on to my virginity had been a choice for me. I didn't want to just have sex with a guy who I wasn't in love with. When I had sex I wanted to know it was the right time. With the right person. Gunner had never been the right person. And I was only fifteen. Other girls were having sex, and I constantly heard how silly I was for waiting and how Gunner was going to cheat on me. But I hadn't cared.

I was waiting.

Until Rhett took that choice away from me that night he took my virginity. I still deal with nightmares about it. But Bryony's birth had changed me a lot. Made me stronger and healed me in a way nothing else could.

I'd decided I was a virgin still. Maybe not physically,

but in my heart. I hadn't chosen to give myself to a guy yet. That choice was still mine to hold on to. I wouldn't allow Rhett to have taken that from me.

"My samich," Bryony said happily and clapped as I set the ketchup-and-toast sandwich in front of her.

"Do I like that?" Grandmamma asked me.

Smiling, I shook my head. I wasn't sure anyone other than a one-year-old could actually like that.

"You like pears and cottage cheese," I reminded her.

She nodded again, then looked behind her. "Have you seen Thomas?"

CHAPTER 6

BRADY

This Friday was the first game in the playoffs. We were all nervous, but the excitement was building. We had a real chance at the championship this year. To go out our senior year as champions would be epic. I had already decided on going to Texas A&M next year. Everyone thought I was going to Alabama, but when the pros and cons were all put in front of me, my future looked better at A&M.

That announcement hadn't happened yet, though. I was waiting until we held the championship in our hands before I said a word. Next year was just that . . . next year. I was focused on the here and now. Getting my head distracted by what could happen next year didn't help us win games.

Turning the aisle at the grocery store with the gallon of milk Mom had sent me to get, I came face-to-face with Lyla Young. Riley's mother.

"Well, hello, Brady. You've grown two feet since I saw you last. Hard to believe you're all seniors this year."

The Youngs had always been good parents. Like my own. They held barbecues and parties for our group of friends over the years and were involved in the school functions. Or they had been. Before.

"Hello, Mrs. Young. Good to see you," I replied.

She smiled, and it was genuine. Not bitter or angry like I would expect. After all, I was friends with the Lawtons. I had taken their side. I had been happy to see Vance leave town last week. Everyone said he was a ticking time bomb. I wasn't a family friend. At least not anymore.

"Tell Coralee I said hello."

"Yes, ma'am," I replied. Then for some reason I can't explain I blurted out, "I saw Riley and her daughter yesterday." Why those words came out of my mouth I wasn't sure, and I would do anything to cram them back in and walk away.

Lyla smiled. "That Bryony is a sweetheart. Riley is so good with her. I hope you said hello."

Again, no judgment or anger in her words. She was sincere. Mom had always liked Lyla.

"I gave them a ride. It was storming and they looked to be out for a walk."

"Oh yes, they walk to the park every day when I get off work. Riley stays with her grandmother until I can get home to take care of her. Bryony loves the outdoors, so Riley likes to get her out every day."

Even though everything in me hadn't believed Riley two years ago, right now I believed her mother. Riley did appear to be a good mom. And the little girl had loved her. She was taking care of her grandmother, too. The doubt was there now. What if we'd all been wrong?

"You take care, now. I've got to get home and start supper. It's time for Riley to do her online schooling, so I'll need to watch Bryony for her. Don't forget to tell your mother I said hello," she said with a wave, then went past me.

I didn't move right away. My brain was going in several directions. More than that, though, there was a sick knot in my stomach. The person who had suffered hadn't deserved to at all.

Finally I turned and headed for the checkout with my milk. I had a football game to concentrate on, but how could I? When Riley Young was taking online courses, raising her daughter, and caring for her grandmother while the town shunned her?

I needed to go talk to Riley. I had to clear my head and my conscience. Maybe she was ready to tell the truth. She'd changed, obviously. This new Riley might just tell me we were right. That she'd accused Rhett unfairly.

Pulling out my phone, I sent a text to Nash letting him know I needed to cancel tonight's plans to watch game clips. We needed the whole team together anyway for it to do any good. I'd get them all together tomorrow night.

Then I scrolled through my contacts to see if Riley's number was still there. It was. Chances were the number had changed, but I thought I'd give it a chance. I paid for the milk, then headed outside with the phone pressed to my ear.

The "number you are trying to reach is no longer in service" message came through like I'd expected, and I ended the call and put the phone back in my pocket. Only other option was to go by her grandmother's. I'd do that after dinner.

Worst that could happen would be that she wouldn't want to talk to me. But knowing Riley, I doubted it. Confrontation was obviously something she handled well. She'd taken on the whole town when she'd accused Rhett.

Words my mom had said when it all happened still rang in my head. *It sure takes a lot of guts for a girl to accuse a guy of rape. Especially a Lawton. Don't see why she'd tell that if it wasn't the truth. Think about that before you jump to his defense.*

I had chalked it up to my mother liking Lyla. But there was a truth to her words. They made sense. So if she was right—if Riley wasn't lying—then what?

The guilt of that possibly being true almost kept me from going. Almost.

My need to know the truth outweighed my fear we could have all been wrong.

If I didn't have the milk, I would go talk to her now. But it was time for Mom to cook dinner, and she needed milk. I'd have to wait.

CHAPTER 7

RILEY

I had just tucked Bryony into bed when the doorbell rang. This was the only time of the day I got to take a break. I didn't have to take care of Grandmamma, and my school-work was finished. I would have a few hours to myself before I went to sleep. So the doorbell ringing meant company, and I didn't want anyone visiting.

Yes, that sounded selfish, because it was probably someone here to check on Grandmamma, but I was just being honest. I wanted peace and quiet. It was what helped me unwind.

"Riley, it's for you," my mother's voice called out. That I hadn't been expecting. I never got company. Ever.

"What?" I replied, thinking I had heard her wrong.

"You have a visitor," she replied.

Okay, well, then maybe I *had* heard her correctly. Who in the world would visit me? I knew it wasn't a Lawton, because if it were, my mother wouldn't be so calm. They'd never get through the door. I was almost positive there would be yelling. I headed for the door, trying to guess who this could be, but no one came to mind. When I turned the corner and saw Brady Higgens standing in the living room, I froze. Why was Brady here?

"Look how tall he's gotten," Mom said, smiling as if his visit were the best thing in the world. She didn't realize he was here to talk about Bryony and what he had heard. She thought he was being friendly. Everyone always thought Brady was just being the nice guy.

"Why are you here?" I asked, not wanting to do the small-talk thing.

"Riley." Mother's tone was that of a warning. But I just didn't care.

"I'd like to talk, about things," he said in his *I'm nice, just trust me* voice.

"It's not your concern," I snapped back at him. He was Gunner Lawton's friend. They were tight, and I didn't trust him at all.

"Riley," Mother said, trying to get my attention. I was

ignoring her. This was my problem. She needed to back out of it.

"It's okay, Mrs. Young. I deserve this. I wasn't nice to Riley two years ago, and I took the Lawtons' side," he said, glancing at my mom, then back to me. "But I'd like to talk to you now. Understand. Listen."

I didn't need him to understand or listen. Who the hell did he think he was? I would ask him just that if it wouldn't send my mother into a fit.

"My life is good. I don't care what you or anyone else thinks or believes. I stopped trying to convince anyone of anything a long time ago. Just leave. Let me be."

"Riley, that's enough. I'd like to speak to you in the kitchen," my mother said in a stern voice. I wanted to tell her no, but I wasn't stupid.

I spun around on my heel and stalked to the kitchen. She whispered something to Brady and I rolled my eyes. She was buying his nice-guy shit just like everyone else. Ugh. It made me sick.

"I cannot believe the way you are acting. That boy came here because he believes you. He saw Bryony and he wants to talk to you. Make amends. Why can't you let him? He could be a good friend. You say you don't need friends, but you do! You more than anyone I know needs a friend. That boy in there is a good one."

My face felt hot from the anger boiling inside me. "That boy in there," I snarled, pointing my finger in the direction of the living room, "turned on me and called me a liar two years ago. He was supposed to be my friend, but he never listened to me. No one here did. Why would you think I'd give him a chance now? Because he wants his conscience cleared? Well, boo-freaking-hoo. I do not feel bad for him."

Mom shook her head and dropped her hands from her hips, but there was a softness in her eyes. "Honestly, Riley, when are you going to let all this pain and bitterness go? Yes, you were hurt in the worst possible way, and it breaks my heart to think about it. But you were given a beautiful gift from it all. You know that. You're a wonderful mom and you are so strong. But you are holding on to this pain and keeping others out. That's not a good example for Bryony. You need a friend, sweetheart. It's time to let someone in, and from all I know of Brady Higgens, he's a really good kid."

Well, crap. That was low. Bringing Bryony into it. I made sure never to let her ears hear about the past and what I went through. I wanted her safe from all that. I did everything I could to make her life happy and complete.

"That's not fair. Bryony doesn't know any of this."

Mom shrugged. "Maybe not, but she sees your body language. She will one day realize that you're carrying bitterness and hurt. And that you build walls around your-self. She'll learn to do the same."

That was what broke me. If she was right, and my mother was rarely wrong, I couldn't live with myself. I was in self-preserve mode. It wasn't an easy life, but after what I'd been through, it was the only way I could deal. I didn't trust easily. Or at all. But that didn't mean I wanted Bryony to live like me.

"But why Brady? How does my telling him anything change that? He's not going to become my buddy. He's got a football team to worry about, and a college scholarship. My talking to him does nothing."

But ease his guilt, I finished in my head. Which I still thought was unfair. I wanted him to feel guilty. He should.

"You don't know that. Give him a chance," my mother replied.

I'd go listen to him simply because if I didn't, my mother wouldn't shut up about it for weeks. Possibly months. I didn't want to hear Brady Higgens's name again after tonight. He might not be at the top of the list of the people I hated, but he was on the list.

"Fine," I sighed in defeat and turned to go back to the living room, hoping Brady had just left.

He hadn't.

There he stood with his hands in his jeans pockets,

looking my way. Our eyes locked, and I saw uncertainty there. He still wasn't sure if he believed me. I didn't care if he did. I didn't care if anyone did. That was all history.

"We can talk, but not here. I don't want Bryony waking up and hearing anything."

He nodded. "Understood. Want to take a drive?"

No. I wanted to go soak in a bath and forget he had come over.

Continue On with Your
Crown of Sainthood

CHAPTER 8

BRADY

Riley looked like she was preparing to walk through a fire. She did not want to be out here with me, and she definitely didn't want to be getting in my truck. I'd heard most of their conversation through the thin walls. Not that I was trying to, but Riley was talking loud, and she had been pissed.

The way she had talked made me believe her even more. That had been as convincing as it got. She had moved on and wanted to put this behind her. The fact that her mother said she needed a friend made my chest hurt. I'd never been without a friend. But Riley had lived the past two years without one.

I went to open her door for her, and she jerked around and glared at me. "I can open it."

Okay, then. Apparently my mother was wrong. Opening car doors for females didn't make them melt. At least not all of them. It pissed this one off.

She climbed inside and slammed the door before I even got to the driver's side. Once I was inside she turned her head to look at me. "Let's get this straight. I'm doing this to shut my mother up. You do not deserve this. I shouldn't have to sit through it. But I am. If I don't, my mom will nag me about it for weeks. I don't have the time to listen to that. So get to the point. We can do it sitting right here. This shouldn't be a long conversation."

I thought about ignoring that and starting my truck, but I decided against it. Being seen driving around with Riley in my truck would lead to questions I didn't want to answer. People seeing my truck in their driveway was easier to explain. I could say my mom sent me over with food for the family since they're having a tough time with her grandmamma. That was believable.

Did that make me sound like a wuss? Yes, it did, but one thing at a time. I was here and that was something.

"I was still fourteen when all of this happened. Which made me young and stupid. I believed Rhett because he was my friend's older brother, and the rest of the town was so outraged I figured they must be right. I didn't question it. And . . . maybe I should have."

She let out a short, hard laugh. "Maybe you should have." She repeated my words and laughed again. "I seriously don't have time for this," she said as she reached for her door handle.

"Wait. Please. Just . . . give me a minute. I'm trying to say this right."

Sighing, she dropped her hand from the handle. I had a small window of opportunity here. She was no longer interested in getting people to believe her. That much was obvious.

"Let me ask you something, Brady. Why are you having a change of heart? Because you saw Bryony? Because wouldn't the girl you all assumed I was when I left town have slept with any guy from here to Arkansas to get knocked up?"

She was giving me an opening. I took it. "No. Because seeing you with her made me question everything. You're a good mom. Bryony loves you. You're taking care of your grandmother, homeschooling to get your diploma, and you could have given her up for adoption or even aborted her, but you didn't. All those things say a lot about your character. They don't say you're a lying, careless manipulator."

There. I'd said everything I was thinking.

She didn't reply right away. I was preparing myself for some smart comment, but it didn't come. Instead she stared out the window toward her house. I waited for her to either try and leave again or say something.

"I've told the story so many times I'm sick of telling it. No one believed me but my parents and the police. And then the Lawtons got in the officer's ear, and he turned on me too. I was young and terrified of sex. Why would I lie about it? That's what I never understood," she said before turning to look back at me.

"You know the story, Brady. You heard it two years ago like everyone else. It hasn't changed. But I have. I'm not naïve anymore. I grew up."

I believed her. Every word. The pain in her eyes was clear even with nothing but the streetlight illuminating her face. The guilt inside me grew, and I wanted to hug her or apologize or do something, but she wouldn't accept it.

"I'm sorry," I finally said.

She gave me a small half smile that tilted up one corner of her mouth. "Yeah, well, you're the only one."

And she was right. I was the only one. The others would believe Rhett forever. It made me sick to think about how power and popularity could ruin others' lives.

"If I could convince them, I would," I told her honestly.

She laughed again and shook her head. "If anyone else

said that, I wouldn't believe them. But you've always been the hero. Continue on with your crown of sainthood and go about your life. I made it through hell and was rewarded with that little girl sleeping in there. She's all I need."

When she reached for the door this time, I didn't ask her to stop. My question had been answered. My guilt wasn't relieved, and I knew it never would be. Just like she would never forget the pain this town put her through.

"If you ever need a friend, I'm here," I told her as she stepped out of the truck.

She didn't laugh this time, but I could see a smile that didn't reach her eyes. "Sure you are, Brady. But I'm not a charity case. I'm strong, and I don't need anyone."

As she walked back to the house, I watched until she was safely inside before I started my truck. Tonight I hadn't made myself feel better, and I realized that was exactly why I had come here to begin with. I had wanted to ease my mind.

It had done the opposite.

I was more weighed down than before. Riley was a good person. Life had been unfair to her. This town had been unfair to her. She'd been raped by an older guy, then ridiculed when she needed support. I had been one of those who turned on her. I couldn't change the past, but I was going to change the future.

Riley Young was going to be my friend. I wasn't sure

how I would make this happen, because she obviously didn't like me. Hell, I doubted she had even an ounce of respect for me. But I would make it my mission to earn her friendship just like I had earned her hate. The girl we had all turned against hadn't crumbled. She had found a strength inside herself and survived. I admired that. I wanted to believe I was that strong. But if I was faced with a real crisis in my life, would I be able to overcome it like she had? I didn't want to doubt it, but I did.

Human Nature Isn't
Always Pretty

CHAPTER 9

RILEY

Mom was smiling at me when I walked back into the house. She thought she had achieved something. All she'd achieved was Brady getting to ease some guilt. I'd probably never see him again unless it was in passing when I was walking Bryony to the park. He had his answers. He believed me. But it meant nothing to me.

"Well," Mom said as she stared at me.

"I'm sure Brady will get a good night's sleep tonight. His football career is safe. Sir Lancelot can continue on his merry way, bringing joy to all," I replied with a fake cheer in my voice.

Mom's smile fell into a frown. "Honestly, Riley, that's not a healthy attitude. It took a lot of nerve for him to come here and talk to you. He's the first one of your friends to believe you. That says a lot."

I stopped walking toward the hallway and turned back around. "My friends? Are you serious, Mom? They aren't my friends. They were never my friends. Friends don't turn on you like that. I have never had real friends. Ever."

"Honey, y'all were young," she started, and I held up my hand to stop her.

"No. Do not say that. We weren't that young. We were going into the tenth grade. They all called me a liar. All of them. When I was hurt and terrified, they turned on me. All I had was you and Dad. I do not have friends. I never have," I repeated.

Mom leaned back on the sofa, resigned. "Okay" was her simple response. "I understand why you feel that way. I would too in your situation. Honestly when it all happened I felt like I didn't have friends either. Everyone was different with me. As if they questioned your story too. It hurt, but I can't imagine how much more it hurt you. If you aren't ready for a friend or to trust someone, I understand. But one day you're going to have to, Riley. One day you are going to need the courage to step out and let someone in. Human nature isn't always pretty. You saw a very ugly side of it at a young age."

This wasn't the first time we'd had this conversation. But it had been a while. A year ago, a guy in the town we were living had asked me out on a date. He worked at the local movie theater, and I went there once a week to watch a movie after Bryony went to bed at night.

I had stopped going to the movies after that. The idea of facing him or even trusting someone wasn't something I wanted to do. I didn't desire the things I once had. I hadn't wanted to date or get close to anyone.

Mom didn't get it. No one got it. I was tired of trying to get them to understand. I just needed to be left alone. I liked things as they were. Changing them now was point- less. I had a rhythm. Bryony was happy with our routine. My life as a social teen was over. I was a mom.

Why couldn't she just be happy for me? I had a plan for my future. Not all seventeen-year-olds could say that. I didn't rely on a guy to make me feel important. That was also a solid check in my corner. So why did my mother think I still needed fixing? I was pretty damn perfect like this.

"Good night, Mom," I said before heading down the hallway to the bathroom. Where I would soak in the tub for an hour and read a book. That was all I needed tonight. I didn't need friends. I had Bryony. She was my world.

"Momma." Bryony's soft voice was in my ear. "Momma."

I opened my eyes to see my daughter hovering over my face.

Stretching my hands over my head, I smiled up at her. "Good morning," I said.

"Gan'mamma gone," she replied, frowning.

That took me only a second to sink in before I sat up and swung my feet over the side of the bed and jumped up. Bryony scrambled down beside me.

"Do you mean she left the house?" I asked her.

Bryony nodded. "Her go park?" she asked hopefully. Bryony woke up wanting to go to the park. It was a daily thing. I hoped I was misunderstanding her and my grandmother was still in this house. My heart was beating frantically regardless as I jerked on a pair of shorts and ran down the hallway toward the kitchen.

"Grandmamma!" I called out loud enough so I she could hear me anywhere in the house.

No response. "Grandmamma!"

Why hadn't Mom woken me up this morning? This wouldn't have happened if I had been awake.

"Gan'mamma," Bryony called out behind me. "You go park?"

I turned to look in the living room, and the front door was wide open.

"Oh God," I whispered then reached for Bryony, picking her up and running outside at the same time.

This could not be happening. My grandmother could

have gone anywhere. She couldn't remember anything, much less directions. And I was supposed to be watching her. Why had I slept late?

I buckled Bryony into her stroller. She was still in her pajamas and needed a diaper change, but there was no time for that. I had to find my grandmother.

I shared a car with my mom. She had it at work this morning. So we would have to search on foot. My phone was still inside, beside the bed, and I would have to leave it there because there was no time to lose. Running barefoot in the tank top that I'd slept in and a pair of cut-off jean shorts, I ran toward the street pushing Bryony.

Stopping, I looked both ways, not sure which way to go first.

"Dat way, Momma," Bryony said, pointing to the right toward town.

"Did you see her leave?" I asked Bryony.

She nodded. "Gan'mamma dat way."

I kissed her little blond head in gratitude and started running down the sidewalk toward town, praying I found her before something bad happened. I would set my alarm for five in the morning from now on. Never again would this happen. Never again.

We've Got Workout in
Five Minutes
CHAPTER 10

BRADY

As I reached for my protein shake, something caught my eye and I slowed my truck down. It was Riley and Bryony running down the street. I turned back around at the stop sign. That hadn't looked like a morning exercise run, and I knew Riley stayed with her grandmother in the mornings. Especially this early. It wasn't even seven yet.

Pulling up beside them, I rolled down my window. "Everything okay?" I asked.

Riley turned her head toward me, and there was a frantic look in her eyes. "No, my grandmother is missing."

Shit.

"Get in," I told her. "I'll help you look."

She shook her head. "That's not safe for Bryony. She should really be in a car seat."

Good point. It wasn't raining today, and the threat of lightning didn't outweigh the need for car safety. So I pulled ahead into the service station and parked the truck. Then I ran over to catch up with her.

"What are you doing?" she asked, sounding frustrated.

"I'm going to help you look. Where have you already searched and where should I go check?"

She stopped running then and took several deep breaths. "Why are you doing this?"

"Because your grandmother has Alzheimer's and is missing. You need help finding her." I would have thought the answer was obvious.

"Someone could see you with me. It's that time of day when everyone is headed to school."

"Where do I look, Riley?" I repeated, annoyed with her comment. I understood why she thought that, but it stung to hear her say it. I didn't want to be that guy. The one who cared what everyone else thought.

"Fine. I was going to the park because Bryony thinks she may be there. Could you go to the grocery store?"

"On it. I'll meet you back at the park," I told her and took off running in the direction of the grocery store. I wondered if she'd called her parents yet. If we didn't find her grandmother in the next fifteen minutes, I would ask.

The manager, Mr. Hart, saw me run inside and smiled. "Need something this early?" he asked.

I shook my head. "No, Mrs.—uh, Lyla Young's mother is missing. Have you seen her in here this morning?"

Mr. Hart's eyes went wide. "Amelia? Good Lord, she has Alzheimer's" was his response.

"Yeah, she does. Have you seen her?"

He shook his head. "No, but I'll make some calls and keep my eyes open."

"Thanks," I replied then hurried back out the door and headed for the park. Maybe the little girl had guessed right. I sure hoped so.

"Brady! Man, what are you doing? We got workout in five minutes," West called out from his truck.

"I'm helping Riley find her grandmother. She's missing. Tell Coach I'm sorry and I'll be there soon as we find her."

West frowned. "Riley Young?" he asked as if I had just said something insane.

"Yeah," I replied and kept running. I didn't have time to defend myself. He could be judgmental if he wanted to. That was something I was going to have to deal with if Riley ever decided to let me be her friend.

"Doesn't her grandmother have Alzheimer's?" he called out after me.

"Yeah, she does."

I didn't look back as I answered.

It wasn't until I got to the park to see Riley running back out of it while pushing the stroller that I heard footsteps behind me.

I turned to see West. *What the hell?*

"What are you doing?" I asked, confused.

"Helping. Where have y'all not looked?" he asked.

This was a turn of events I didn't expect. "Only checked the park and grocery store."

Riley looked even more terrified than she had when I first saw her. "She's not there," she said, her gaze darting to West then back to me.

"Mr. Hart is looking around for her too. He'll have the whole town aware she's missing in no time. Have you told your mom?"

She shook her head. "No. I left my phone at the house because I was in such a big rush."

I slid my phone out of my pocket and handed it to her. "You'd better call."

She took the phone, then I turned back to West. "Go check the post office and ask at the pharmacy," I told him.

He nodded and turned to jog toward the main street.

"Why's he here?" she asked, frowning.

"He stopped to help."

She looked as surprised as I had been. I had a feeling Maggie was to thank for his help. The West before Maggie wouldn't have stopped. He'd have told me I was an idiot and gone to practice.

"Mom, it's me. I'm using Brady's phone. No, he's not at the house. No, I'm not. That's the thing. No. Just listen. She's missing, Mom. I woke up before seven and the front door was open." Tears filled her eyes. "And we're looking for her."

She sniffled and wiped at the tears beginning to roll down her face. "Yes. The park, the grocery, and West is checking the post office and the pharmacy."

She paused and her gaze jerked back up to meet mine. There was hope there. "I hadn't thought of that. We'll go there now. Okay, I will."

She hung up and handed me the phone. "The church. She went missing once before, right after we moved back here. It was when we realized she could never be left alone. She went to the church, then forgot where she was and why she was there."

She began pushing the stroller and running again.

"You run and I'll push the stroller. We will follow," I told her, knowing she needed to get to the church.

"Thank you," she said as she bent down to kiss Bryony on the head and told her to be good and that she'd be right ahead of us.

She was off sprinting toward the small Baptist church in town. It was one of three churches. At least they knew which church to check. I followed quickly behind her, hoping we found her grandmother and she was all right.

CHAPTER 11

RILEY

Her white hair was the first thing I saw as I ran up the church steps. She was out at the cemetery to the left of the building. I turned and made my way back down the steps and out to where she was wandering around. The relief at seeing her made my eyes fill up with more tears. My heart was still racing, and I doubted that would slow down quickly.

"Grandmamma," I called out, not wanting to startle her.

She paused and looked up at me, her eyes full of the confusion I so often saw there. She didn't respond but continued to watch me.

"Grandmamma, what are you doing?" I asked, careful not to scold her for leaving the house because the doctors said she wouldn't understand when she did something wrong or remember it next time.

"I think . . . ," she began, then trailed off and let her gaze scan the graves around her like she wasn't sure what she thought.

"Did you get lost?" I asked trying to sound casual and not frantic.

She turned back to me and nodded.

"Well, good news is I'm here to take you home. Mom will be here in just a minute and she'll give us a ride. Then I can make you some breakfast. Don't you want something to eat? You've got to be starving."

Again she nodded.

I heard Bryony call, "Momma," from behind me and I let out another sigh to try and calm myself before turning to her and Brady. I owed him a big thank-you for helping. It wasn't expected.

"The baby's here," Grandmamma said.

"Yes, she's here too."

"She needs to eat breakfast. I was going to fix her oats and strawberries," Grandmamma said.

"That's a good idea. We need to get home first, though."

Brady and Bryony stopped beside me, and I smiled at him. "Thank you for your help. She's okay," I told him, although that was kind of obvious.

He nodded. "I'm glad. I'll go tell West. Do you need a ride or anything?"

I shook my head. "Mom's on her way."

"Okay. Well, I'll see you around," he said, then gave my grandmother a smile before leaving us there and heading back toward town and his truck.

"Bye-bye," Bryony called out after him.

He paused, then turned back and flashed her with a grin that I will admit was hard not to get a little fluttery over. Then he waved at her before once again walking away.

"Why are we here?" Grandmamma asked me.

"I think you must have come out for a morning walk and didn't tell me. We don't need to do that anymore. If you want to walk, I will go with you," I told her, knowing that was pointless. She'd forget this happened any minute now.

"Go to pawk." Bryony added her suggestion with a clap of her hands. She'd not been happy that we had gone to the park and not stayed.

"Later today. First we have breakfast to cook. Aren't you hungry?"

That got her attention. She nodded her head just as Mom pulled up.

I didn't let Grandmamma out of my sight for the rest of the morning. From now on, Mom agreed she'd make sure

I was awake and out of bed before she left the house. By the time I was able to take Bryony to the park I was so emotionally exhausted that all I did was sit and watch her play. I normally played with her, but today I didn't have it in me. I just needed to sit and stare.

Several things had been running through my head since this morning's scare. First of all, Brady helping me like he did. I had said I didn't need a friend, but today I'd needed one, and he had come through.

Second, the fact that West had jumped in to help. West Ashby wasn't known for his chivalry. I wasn't sure what had gotten into him. I knew Brady had power with the football team, but from what I remember, West Ashby wasn't one to easily be swayed. He hated me. Just like the rest of Lawton High School.

And this town.

Bryony had taken a liking to Brady. That wasn't unusual, though. She liked just about everyone. Still, hearing her tell him bye today had struck a chord with me. Could I be friends with him? Did he actually want that? Did *I* actually want that?

"How are things at home? Is your grandmother okay after this morning's excitement?" Brady's voice interrupted my thoughts.

I blinked several times to get out of the trance I had

been in, then turned my head back to look up at him. "She's good," I replied, not realizing Brady had walked up to the bench I was sitting on.

He glanced over at the slide where Bryony was playing. "I think she enjoyed the outing this morning, at least."

She had. Bryony had seen it as one big adventure. "It was a game of hide-and-seek for her," I agreed.

He shifted his feet, and the awkward silence that fell made me once again question what he was doing here. Had he come looking for me? It was after school, but I assumed he would have practice.

"So are you coming to the game Friday night?" he asked.

Was he an idiot? "Um, no," I said. "You do remember who I am, right?"

He sighed and tucked his hands in his pockets. "It's been two years. Things have changed at the Lawton house."

I'd heard about those changes. At least what the rest of the town knew. I was sure Brady probably knew a lot more. The little I had heard talk about, Gunner was living in that big house alone. The owner. He'd inherited it all, and his dad had left town. I wasn't sure where his mother was.

"Trust me, two years means nothing in this town," I told him.

He didn't respond right away, and I figured he knew I was right. It was how small towns worked. There was always a villain everyone was against. I was that person. The teenage girl who'd had a child at fifteen, hated because she'd simply told the truth.

"Maybe if you got out more and tried," he suggested.

I just laughed. "Tried what exactly?" I had been hated by these people. They still turned their heads when I walked by them and acted as if they didn't know me. Then there were the ones who looked at me with disgust or, even worse, pity. I didn't want their self-righteous pity.

He didn't have an answer for that. In the end he nodded. "Guess you're right." Then he waved at Bryony, who had noticed him, before saying, "See you around." I watched him leave, and a part of me wished his suggestion were possible. Which was stupid, I knew. I had decided long ago I didn't care what this town thought of me.

However, I missed having a friend my age. Brady had reminded me of that. His coming around was nice. But forgetting how he had turned on me was difficult. It made things complicated. Just because his charming smile and disregard for what people thought was endearing didn't mean I could start trusting him.

Two years ago . . .
Spend-the-night parties at Ivy's always
ended this way. Kimmie would call boys,

they'd come over, Serena and Kimmie would sneak out, and Ivy would go crying to her parents. Why I continued to come to these things, I didn't know. Gunner had laughed at me when I told him I was going to this one tonight. His prediction that I wouldn't stay may have been spot-on.

Ivy came back to her room sniffling while Naomi and Hillary looked nervously at each other. We were never sure what to expect with Ivy's theatrics.

"Mom said y'all can stay. She's calling their parents, though. They'll never get invited here again."

We all sat silently, but we knew that wasn't the truth. Ivy wanted to be friends with Serena. She craved the popularity that came with being attached to Serena. I, for one, didn't think it was so grand to be popular just because you had a certain reputation among guys. But Ivy apparently didn't get that.

"I'm sorry, Ivy," Hillary said, walking over to her to hug her. She was acting like her dog had just died. Seriously? We had these parties about once a month, and every time we did, those two ran off with boys. Why were we acting like this was a surprise?

"They did this the last three times you've had one of these this year. Why don't you just stop inviting them?" I said, rolling my eyes and lying back on the sleeping bag I'd brought with me. I was debating walking home and waking up my parents with ringing the doorbell. If they were going to baby Ivy all night over this, I would. We were going into the tenth grade in a week. It was time everyone acted like it.

"Don't be mean, Riley," Hillary scolded me. "Ivy tries to include everyone."

That was such a hilarious lie I almost laughed out loud. Ivy most certainly didn't deserve the Mother Teresa award. The only reason that Naomi had been invited this time was that she had started dating West Ashby last week. Ivy only invited people she thought were important. I had been friends with Ivy since preschool, and I knew Ivy didn't include "everyone."

I considered pointing out that the only

reason Hillary was here was because she'd had a summer romance with Brady Higgens and Ivy had her eye on Brady. Ivy was keeping her enemies close. Poor Hillary didn't realize that, though, and I wasn't going to be the one to tell her.

"Did you see who they left with? Rhett Lawton was driving. He's a senior!" Ivy said in horror. Rhett was my boyfriend's older brother. Serena wanted him bad. Everyone knew it.

"Connor and Joel were with him," Naomi piped up.

Ivy nodded dramatically. "What are they thinking! Those boys only want sex."

"It's Serena's favorite pastime," Hillary said with disgust, although rumor had it she'd slept with Connor two weeks before she'd started dating Brady. I bit my lip to keep from smirking.

I closed my eyes and wondered if we would actually sleep tonight or discuss the wild ways of Serena and Kimmie. My bed really sounded good about now, and I missed it. The older we got, the more I felt

myself wanting to pull away from them.
We weren't little girls anymore. Those
days were gone. There was sex, boys, and
drama in our lives that I wasn't a big fan
of. Yet here I stayed in the middle of it all.
Listening.

CHAPTER 12

BRADY

West was standing out by his truck when I pulled into the driveway. He was either waiting on Maggie or he was waiting on me. The frown between his eyebrows said it was me. He never frowned at Maggie.

"What's up?" I called out as I walked around the front of my truck.

"I was going to ask you the same thing," he replied. "Didn't want to bring it up at practice, but this Riley thing. I get why you were helping today, but I also know your truck was seen at her grandmother's last night. That hasn't reached Gunner's ears yet, but when it does, you ready to explain that?"

It had been two years, but this grudge was still holding strong. The more time I spent around Riley, the more I believed she'd been treated unfairly. That this town should have listened to her, not ridiculed her.

"Not sure I believe Rhett was innocent. Not anymore. Not after the way we saw him act just last month."

West nodded slowly, but his frown stayed in place. "Maybe. But we have a championship to win. If Gunner still believes his brother and you're hanging around Riley, then we are going to have a problem. Don't know what I believe anymore, but I do know that this isn't the time to make any bold statements."

I understood what he was saying. It wasn't as if Riley was going to warm up to me any time soon anyway. I'd tried to be her friend, but she wasn't interested. We had the biggest game in our high school career, the state championship, coming up in a few weeks, and we had to actually get there by winning the last two games that would place us at that game. If we lost, our season ended. We had to win the play-offs to get to the championship game.

"You're right," I replied. "I won't be seen with her anymore. This morning was a fluke. That's all."

The front door opened and Maggie stepped out. She was dressed like they were going somewhere: in a yellow sundress, with her hair curled. "Looks like you got a date."

West turned and his face went from serious to love-struck. If Maggie weren't my cousin, I would laugh at him. But Maggie had lived through hell, and she'd found happiness with West. The most unlikely guy in the world to end up saving her.

"Yeah, I do," he agreed, then walked toward her. He'd forgotten me and our conversation. For now.

I waved at Maggie and told them to have a good time before heading inside. The smell of Mom's meat loaf engulfed me as I walked into the house. I knew she'd have creamed potatoes, turnip greens, and corn bread to go with it. Dropping my bag by the front door, I headed for the kitchen.

"He's home. Let's eat," my dad said, turning to look at me with a large mason jar full of sweet tea in his hand.

Mom chuckled and shook her head. "The man has no patience. I've been slapping his hand away from the meat loaf since he walked in the door. First night home for dinner in a week, and he acts like this."

Dad had been working on a project at work that was keeping him late every evening.

"Smells great. I'm starved. Where's Maggie headed?" I asked, knowing my mother would have the details of their date.

"West is taking her to some fancy place in Franklin. He

got a reservation for it and everything. She spent an hour trying to decide what to wear. I just love watching her like this. Hard to believe four months ago when she moved here she wouldn't even speak."

She had come a long way in a short time. I agreed with Mom there. It was all thanks to West, but then again she'd been West's rock through his father's death too. Really, they'd saved each other.

"Let's talk football," Dad said, not wanting to be reminded of why Maggie was here and why she had come to us not speaking. Maggie's mother was his sister, and her brutal death still haunted him. Mom said he had nightmares about it.

"We look good. Friday night won't be easy, but we should win. As long as everyone keeps their head in the game this week. I thought I'd have the guys over tonight to watch some clips of the Panthers play this year. So we would know what to look for."

"Good idea. West has to have Maggie back by nine. He'll miss most of it," Dad said, sitting down with his plate piled high with food.

"I'll make some cookies," Mom said, then handed me a plate.

"We can do it tonight and tomorrow night for those who can't come tonight. I mentioned it after practice. The guys who are available tonight will be here around seven thirty."

Dad nodded his head as if he approved of the idea. "What does Coach say? He think y'all are ready?"

"You know Coach. He never thinks we're ready. Part of what makes us work. We never get comfortable."

For the rest of dinner we discussed Friday night. It was what we always talked about this time of year. Once the championship was over, we would talk about next year. College football. My future.

Three years ago . . .

"You know your brother is banging Serena. Isn't that, like, illegal?" West asked Gunner.

I had heard that Serena was sneaking around with Rhett too. But I hadn't wanted to bring it up. Leave it to West to throw that out there.

"Naw, he's still seventeen. She doesn't become illegal until his birthday in April."

West laughed. "So he's gonna bang the freshman while he still can. I want to be Rhett when I grow up."

Gunner smirked. "Join the club."

I didn't say anything because I in no

way wanted to be Rhett Lawton. I thought he was cool and I admired his skill on the field, but he was always partying. Dad said I wouldn't make it far in life if I lived like that. I had a future in the NFL to pursue. Rhett was the heir to the Lawton millions. I doubted he planned on any career, really. Other than taking over for his dad one day.

"Y'all want to go outside and throw the ball?" I asked, hoping to change the subject.

West shrugged and reached for his soda and a bag of chips. "I guess."

"All you do is think football," Gunner replied, still lounging on the sofa.

It was my future. Of course that was all I thought about.

CHAPTER 13

RILEY

This was probably stupid. Maybe even the stupidest idea I had ever come up with. I debated going through with it the entire two-mile walk it took me to get from my grandmamma's house to Brady's house. It was late and very dark.

If I believed that Damon Salvatore was real, I wouldn't be out here. Oh, who was I kidding? Yes, I would. Hot vampires aside, it was dark and spooky at eleven in this town. Everyone was in their house and most in bed. Lights were sparse.

The last noise that had made me squeal and jump had been a cat. I was giving myself a pep talk about being silly right up until I turned onto Brady's driveway and paused. Now what? I was here. I knew which window was Brady's. I just had to toss a rock up there and get his attention.

What if he was asleep? Doubtful.

What if he had changed his mind about the being-friends thing? Possible.

Why the heck was I here again? Because I was lonely. Because Brady had tried to be my friend. And if I was honest with myself, I wanted that.

That was just sad. I glanced back at the sidewalk and thought about turning around and going home. He'd never know I was here, and I would have gotten in a good four miles of cardio before bed. No harm done.

Then tomorrow morning I would wake up and do the same thing I did every day. No one to talk to. No one who believed me but my family.

That reminder had me walking the few last steps into his yard. The small, smooth stone in my hand I had picked up along the way was warm now from my tight clutch. I stared down at it and wondered if this was a bad idea for the hundredth time. Once I had been a chance taker. I had liked adventure.

That girl was gone, though. Life had changed me, but now I wanted a bit of her back.

The stone flew from my hands and with a ping hit his

window. I had only picked up one stone. I figured if he didn't get up after one I was taking that as fate and leaving.

A light came on in the dark room and butterflies became bats in my stomach. I had done it. I had to go through with it now. The curtains moved, and the long, dark hair was the first thing I saw. That was not Brady.

I moved fast into the shadows. I couldn't run for the road. Whoever it was would see me in the streetlight. So I ducked behind the hedges in front of their house and held my breath like they could hear me breathing. Which I know was silly because they were on the second floor.

The sound of the window opening made me cringe, and I didn't move a muscle. That had been a girl. If Brady had a girl in his room, then he sure wouldn't let her come to the window. He'd hide her. So who was it?

The cousin. Holy crap, I'd forgotten about the cousin. Mom had told me about his cousin moving in with them. Apparently she'd gotten his room. Why hadn't I thought about that possibility? If you're gonna throw rocks at a window just before midnight, you need to make sure you've got the right window. I was terrible at this.

The sound of the window closing calmed me some, and I let out the breath I'd been holding. I would need to stay here awhile until I was sure she'd walked away from the window before I made a run for the street. I tried not to think about the critters that could be behind this hedge with me. Staying put was the only safe thing to do here.

This was fate's way of telling me that trying to be Brady's friend was a bad idea. I got that now. I appreciate fate stepping in and stopping me from sure disaster. Now if only fate could make sure no animal bit me back here, that would be really awesome.

The front door opened, and I stopped breathing again. This was not good. I should have run when I had the chance. What if it was Brady's dad and he had a gun? I could end up shot. Even if a squirrel decided to bite me, I wasn't moving now. I preferred a squirrel attack to a gunshot. I think.

When I wanted a change and some adventure, this was not what I had in mind. I needed to get out of this alive. I had a kid to raise.

"Hello?" Brady called out, and I let out a small breath. It was Brady, not his dad, and I was sure Brady didn't have a gun. I was going to live.

"Anyone out here?" he asked.

I could ignore him and let him continue his search, or I could come out of the hedges and announce myself. My goal had been to get Brady down here. That was what had happened. Hiding from him seemed silly now.

Instead of chancing the animal attack, I stood up and stepped out of hiding. This was embarrassing, now that I thought about it: coming here at night and throwing a rock at his window. My face was warm, and I was glad the darkness would mask my embarrassment.

"It's me," I said, and he spun around.

"Riley?"

"Yeah."

"What are you doing? Are you okay?"

No, apparently I was warped in the head. This whole idea seemed terrible. I should have stayed at home in bed and not let my need for friends send me out on this wild chase.

"You, uh, changed bedrooms." I couldn't think of anything smarter to say.

He nodded.

"I didn't know—"

"So you came here and threw a rock at my window because . . . ?"

I was an idiot. I needed my head examined. I was desperate and pathetic.

"I want to be friends." There, I said it.

He didn't respond right away. Instead he studied me a moment, then glanced down at his feet before shifting them.

"I believe you—I mean about the Rhett thing. And I meant what I said last night. But . . . we have the next few games and the championship hopefully in our reach. I can't upset the team."

Meaning, he had thought about it and he couldn't be my friend. He was a habitual good guy, but his future was on the line. I could be mad, but I got it. He'd worked for this as long as I had known him.

"Oh, that makes sense. I get it. Sorry I bothered you." I wanted to sprint for the sidewalk. Get as far away from here as possible. I didn't think it could get any more embarrassing, but it just had.

"Wait! Did you walk here?" His voice sounded concerned.

I wish he'd just let me go. But he was, after all, Mr. Nice Guy. "Yeah," I replied, barely glancing back over my shoulder and not stopping.

"It's not safe for you to be out like this. I'll drive you back."

No, no, no. I needed alone time.

"I'm good. Really. Besides, someone may see you."

He sighed loudly. "Don't be like that, Riley. I meant what I said about being friends. It's just better if we wait until the season is over. Then the team can get mad at me."

I really did understand his decision. I got it completely. But I didn't want to talk about it anymore. "Just let me go, Brady."

I kept walking and only got a little farther before I heard him jogging up behind me. His conscience couldn't handle this. There weren't many guys like Brady Higgens on this earth.

"Then I'm walking you back," he said as he came up beside me. "Would be easier if I drove you, but if you insist on walking, then we will walk."

Stubborn. I stopped and turned to him. "Why can't you just be like every other guy and go back inside and forget I came over here? Or better yet, make fun of me tomorrow to your friends?"

"I'm not every other guy."

No, he wasn't.

I glanced back at his driveway. "Fine. I'll let you give me a ride."

A small smile tugged at his lips. "Thanks."

CHAPTER 14

BRADY

Sleep never came last night, and I felt like shit. Our game was tomorrow, and I had to get my head clear and focused. Problem was, all I could do was remember Riley's face and how hurt she'd been. It was eating me alive.

She had been raped and called a liar, then run out of town. Now she was back because of her grandmother and facing an entire town that didn't welcome her. My grand idea to be her friend had seemed like a good one until I talked to West and he reminded me how bad that could be for the team. West may understand, but Gunner wouldn't. And a lot of people would side with Gunner. The team would be split, and we couldn't win games like that.

"You look terrible," Maggie said as she walked into the kitchen. "Anything to do with the rock at the window last night?"

When Riley had thrown the rock, Maggie had come to get me, figuring that it had been meant for me. I hadn't told her about it when I got back from taking Riley home last night.

"Yeah" was all I said.

"Who's the girl?" Maggie asked, handing me the box of cereal.

"You don't know her."

"Oh, so it was Riley Young."

This town had a big mouth. Jesus.

"That can't get out, Maggie," I said, taking the cereal from her.

"Who am I gonna tell? I'm not exactly a gossip."

She had a point. Although she was talking now, she still didn't talk to many people. She kept a small circle of those she conversed with. Maggie didn't trust easily. Can't say I blame her.

"I know. It's just there is so much drama there. I need to get through the next few weeks without that."

She lifted a shoulder in acknowledgment and took a bite of her cereal. I could see she didn't actually agree with me. She was thinking something else.

"What?" I asked.

"Nothing," she replied.

"Say it."

"Okay, fine. She trusted you, so you did something to gain her trust. I think that her coming here means she needs someone right now."

And I should be that someone. Maggie didn't have to say it. I got what she meant.

"It's complicated."

"She's got a baby, right? She's seventeen and the father claims she's a liar. Sounds like her life is a lot more complicated than yours."

Maggie set her bowl down in the sink and grabbed her book bag. "West just drove up. See you at school."

I finished my cereal, although now it tasted like sawdust. Damn, she was right.

The hallway was filled with people I knew and some I really didn't. I watched them talk and laugh. Friends whispered, and guys called out my name in greeting. It was all very normal. Part of high school life. The last year I'd have this.

All I could think was Riley didn't get this. She was missing it all. My chest felt heavy as I made my way through the crowd of people. Each one I'd seen at some point in my past. I didn't kid myself and believe that none of them had bad things in their lives. We all did.

It was just that they all had someone. They had a place to go. They had people to talk to and escape from reality.

Riley didn't. But she'd trusted me, and I was a dick.

There, I admitted it. I was a complete dick last night.

Figuring out how to fix it, though, was the problem.

"You look lost," Gunner said as he and Willa walked up to me.

I shrugged. I was, but that wasn't something I could talk to him about. "Didn't get much sleep."

Gunner nodded like he understood. He assumed it was the game. And part of it was. Just not the main part.

"I've got to get to class early and go over my study guide for the test. Y'all can talk football," Willa said and kissed Gunner's cheek before leaving us there. Gunner watched her go like he would never see her again, and I figured that had all ended up the way it was supposed to.

The two of them fit in a way we didn't. Besides, I think it had been Gunner for her since we were kids.

"All good in paradise?" I asked him.

He finally glanced back at me. "Yeah. Life isn't shit when she's around."

Gunner had some serious family issues. Willa had been there with him through it all, more so than I could have been.

"I'm glad she came back when she did," I told him honestly.

"Me too," he agreed and turned his head to see her disappear around the corner. "Wish she'd never left."

I wondered if he and Willa would have become a thing earlier if she had stayed here. Maybe he would never have dated Riley, and she'd never have been raped by his brother. Life might have been drastically different for all of them.

"I'm sure she does too," I added.

Gunner shrugged. "Don't know. She made a life for herself there, and although there was a tragic end to it, I don't think she regrets knowing her friend. Even if she had to lose her."

Willa's story wasn't easy either. She'd been through something I hadn't experienced. Having a best friend commit suicide had to have been terrible. But she'd found happiness again.

"West is coming to view the game clips tonight. You in for another round?" I asked him, changing the subject.

"Is your mom making cookies again?"

"Of course."

"Then I'll be there."

I Can See You're Both as
Charming as I Remember

CHAPTER 15

RILEY

With a grocery list in one hand and Bryony's hand in the other, I walked into the store to pick up all the things we needed. Bryony had wanted to go to the park today, but it had rained most of the afternoon, so it was going to be muddy. I'd promised her animal cookies if she was a good girl at the grocery store.

It was a compromise, not a bribe. Or at least I liked to tell myself that.

"Riley *Young*." I recognized the voice. The way my last name was said as if it were distasteful on her tongue made me tense. I hadn't come into contact with Serena since I'd returned. I'd hoped I never would. Apparently my luck had just run out.

I held Bryony close to my side as if they could hurt her, which was silly, but I did it anyway. Turning, I faced not only Serena but Kimmie as well. They looked like older versions of the girls I remembered. Still trying to outdo each other.

"Hello, Serena. Kimmie," I replied with a forced smile.

"You've got a kid. What happened, you didn't use protection?" Kimmie said with a snicker.

I could take them attacking me. But they weren't going to bring Bryony into this.

"I can see you're both as charming as I remember. If you'll excuse me, I have groceries to buy," I replied, wanting to set a good example for my daughter. She was young, but I was still sure she understood things like this. Or they at least made impressions on her.

I walked past them and put Bryony in a buggy.

"Don't forget to grab some condoms. Hate for that to happen again," Serena said with a sweet tone.

I only had so much restraint.

"You're the one who needs to remember her condoms. You wouldn't want to spread around the STDs you've got from years of screwing anyone who would look your way."

With that, I walked off. Maybe it wasn't my finest hour as a mom, but damn, it felt good. They could stew on that and bitch about me for the next week.

"Cookies?" Bryony asked me, and I could see the concerned frown on her face. She hadn't understood what happened, but she was smart enough to know I was rattled.

"Yes, baby girl, we are going to get you cookies," I assured her.

My emotions were too raw from last night's confrontation with Brady. I was being a complete brat about it, but it couldn't be helped. I had trusted him enough to say yes to his offer, then he'd taken it back. I understood his reasons, but it still hurt. That wasn't getting any better.

My life here was for a short time anyway. I would graduate soon, and then I was going to find a job and save up to get me and Bryony a place of our own. I didn't have time for boys and friends. I had a life to build. My teen years were over. They had been since the night I asked Rhett to give me a ride home. Before that night I'd been smarter. I had trusted Brady, who had once been a good friend. Someone I could rely on.

Two years ago . . .
Gunner was drinking again. Being invited
to these field parties early had been our

ultimate goal since we were in elementary school. Thanks to Gunner's older brother and the fact that Gunner was expected to be a future star on the football team, we, along with Brady and West, got to go this summer.

At first, Gunner hadn't drunk with the others. Brady never drank, but West had started sampling the beer. Then Gunner. Now it was a full-on drunk fest. Brady was the only one who remained sober. He was also the one everyone else wanted to talk to. He had started drawing attention from the high school coach two years ago, when he was just in eighth grade. His accuracy with the ball made him important around here.

I sat on an old tractor tire near the fire, where Gunner had been earlier. He'd left me for more to drink and was now laughing with some juniors loudly and annoyingly. I'd liked getting to come to the parties at first, but I wasn't so sure I liked it now. Getting home tonight would be tricky. I couldn't call my mom to come get me because Gunner was hammered. She'd see that.

*I searched the crowd for Rhett, who
normally gave Gunner and me a ride
home. He drank some, but rarely did he
get completely sloshed. I watched him and
decided how safe riding with him would be.
I'd gotten a ride with Brady's mom more
than once. Problem with that was, Brady
stayed until late, and I wasn't in the mood
to stay late.*

*Serena was trying hard to get Rhett's
attention when I found him across the field
by his truck. He seemed more interested
in one of the older girls there. Although
Serena was here because of Rhett, I was
sure. Definitely wouldn't be asking him to
take me home tonight. I guessed I'd have
to suffer through until Brady left. He had a
crowd around him, but I stood up and made
my way over to him anyway. Gunner was
going to be passed out soon, and I needed a
ride home.*

*"Hey, gorgeous," someone called out
with an obvious slur in his voice. I glanced
over to see Ivan, one of Rhett's friends,
walking toward me. The red plastic cup in*

his hand held more than just beer, I'd bet. Ivan had been kicked off the team last year for partying too hard. He rarely showed up for class and was going to flunk out. No one seemed to care about any of this, though. He still hung with the same crowd, and they loved him.

I turned my attention back to Brady's group and hoped Ivan would trip over his drunk feet. "Your boy's not able to handle his beer yet. He leave you all alone? That's a shame. Come over here and we can talk."

Not in this lifetime.

"No thanks," I replied, still not looking at him.

He laughed like that was hilarious. Before he could think of something else to say, I was close enough to Brady that he saw me headed his way. He stopped talking and stepped over toward me.

"You good?" he asked, doing a quick check for Gunner, I assumed.

"Yeah. Just need a ride. Is your mom coming?" I asked.

He nodded, but there was a frown on his face. "Gunner drunk again?"

"Yep."

He shook his head. "I've got to straighten him out. I'll call Mom. We can leave in a few."

"Thanks. I appreciate it."

You Need Rattling
CHAPTER 16

BRADY

Ivy had decorated my locker and left brownies with icing on them inside. She was still acting like we were an item on game days. I didn't want to say something to hurt her feelings, but she had to stop this. We didn't talk the rest of the week. Her mom's brownies were good and all, but they weren't going to fix us. We'd never been right to begin with.

I ate two brownies and drank a large glass of milk before going upstairs to get my bag. Mom would have washed my uniform and packed things up for me to take to the bus. Tonight was important. Vitally. If we didn't win this game, we were out.

The studying of game tapes and all the extra practice

had made me feel ready. I thought the team was prepared. It wasn't them that was weighing on my mind. Instead it was me. The center of the team. The quarterback. Who needed his head adjusted. I hadn't been able to shake loose Riley's visit the other night. It bothered me that she was hurt. That I had been the one to hurt her.

This wasn't new. I was the nice guy. Not because I was labeled with it but because it was simply who I was. Sometimes I seriously hated it.

However, this Riley thing was different. I was worried about her more so than I'd ever worried about Ivy and her feelings. Ivy and I had been on again off again for almost two years, but I'd never felt as strongly for her as I did about Riley. The only reason that I could think of for this was the little girl. Riley had been handed a raw deal and made the best of it. I respected that.

My bag was sitting on my bed like expected, all packed up for me. Mom wasn't home from work yet, but she'd be at the game along with my dad. They would bring Maggie, and it would be the normal Friday night. Except today, my head was not just on the game the way it always is.

Frustrated, I grabbed my bag and headed back downstairs. I had to deal with this now. We were supposed to be at the field house to load the bus in one hour. Before I went there, I was going to see Riley. If I didn't talk to her and ease my mind, I wasn't sure I could pull tonight off. The Panthers were also undefeated. We had a job on our hands, and I had to be 100 percent.

"You leaving already?" Maggie asked as I passed her bedroom door.

I paused and looked in the room. She was on her bed sitting with her legs crossed and a book open in her lap. The girl read more than anyone I knew.

"Yeah," I replied.

"West went home to take a nap before y'all have to meet to leave."

"I need to go do something," I said, not giving her any more detail.

"Well, good luck tonight."

"Thanks. I need it."

She tilted her head to one side and her dark brown hair fell over one shoulder. "Never heard you say that before."

Because I never felt that before. I had always been focused and confident. Not now.

"I've got a lot on my mind is all."

"Riley Young," Maggie replied. It wasn't a question. It was a statement.

"I don't know what you mean," I said, and started to walk off.

"You've been off since she threw the rock at the window

the other night. You made the wrong decision, and it's haunting you."

This wasn't something I wanted to discuss. I just needed to fix it. "You didn't say anything to West, did you?"

She shook her head. "Not my information to tell."

I really liked that about my cousin. She wasn't a gossip. She kept to herself mostly. No drama or girly stuff to contend with. A lot like Riley, I guess.

"I'm working out what the right thing is. Not just for me but for everyone involved." I wasn't making sense, but that was all I was willing to say.

"I don't know her. But I like her."

"Why?" I asked, curious.

"No girl has ever rattled you like this. Not even Willa. Certainly not Ivy. You need rattling."

No, I needed to be levelheaded and ready to win this game. "I disagree."

Maggie picked her book back up like she was done with this conversation. Which was something I liked about her. She didn't go on and on about a topic I was done discussing.

"I've found that the things that rattle us the most are the ones worth making sacrifices for." She said this without looking up at me.

Damn. That struck a chord.

"Did you make sacrifices for West?" I asked, already knowing the answer.

This time she looked up from her book. "I spoke, Brady. I braved the sound of my own voice."

The reason why that was a sacrifice didn't need explaining. I understood. With a nod of my head, I left her there with her book. She had gained life again when she'd spoken to West. A large part of her that had been missing was filled with new reasons to be happy.

I didn't think I was missing anything. I had great parents, I had good friends, and I was going to play football at an SEC college next year. My life couldn't get much better. Before I picked up Riley and Bryony in my truck the other day, I didn't question any of this. I knew I was solid. I was ready for my future.

Now I wondered if I was just living the easy life. Not facing challenges or really making a mark on anyone. Maggie had been West's rock through a hell I never wanted to imagine. Even as broken as she was, she'd stood by him and become his center. She had done something with her life that meant more than just her happiness. She'd found happiness helping someone else.

Was I happy? This life I had . . . Did it make me happy? Did playing football and being the star at Lawton High really make me happy?

No. It didn't. I wasn't fulfilled.

I was empty. Pointless. I was a vessel to win games at my high school. Girls liked me, and I had my pick if I wanted them. My truck wasn't new, but it was nice and had been given to me without my having to work for it. There was nothing worth mentioning I had done for anyone.

Tossing my bag into the passenger seat of my truck I decided that was over. I wasn't focusing on Brady Higgens anymore. Someone needed me. She needed friendship, and she had come to me. Fuck my friends getting mad. They all needed to wake up and realize that was two years ago and we'd all been wrong. I was worried about winning a championship and there was a single mom who I had once considered a friend reaching out. I wasn't ignoring that. Not for a damn game.

You've Got a
Championship to Win
CHAPTER 17

RILEY

There were painted car windows, blue flags with lions on them, and of course large signs in every yard except ours with LIONS #1. My house wasn't worried about the game. We were the only ones in town without some Lions sign in their yard, and in the next town meeting they could possibly vote to run us out of town . . . again . . . because we've failed to be football obsessed.

Smiling at that thought, I shook my head. It wouldn't happen, of course, but the way they all made over a football game you would think it was the presidential election. Bryony pointed at another car that passed us leaving town for the game. The painted windows and flags flying were fascinating to her. At least they were good for something.

The next vehicle that passed wasn't a painted car. It was Brady Higgens's truck. My chest tightened at the sight, and I began walking faster. Getting home wasn't going to make the reminder of the other night go away, but I could at least get busy with making Bryony a snack and cleaning my closet or something. Anything not to remember the fool I'd made of myself.

Bryony clapped and waved at the next car that drove by. They had a stuffed lion's head on the hood. Not sure how they were making that stay. But it sure made Bryony happy. She'd probably enjoy the games. All the fans cheering and guys running on the field. I'd never be able to take her, though. That was a part of my life that was over.

I turned into my grandmamma's drive just as Brady's truck came to a rolling stop beside me. Bryony was waving at him as if he were her best friend. I had already been rude in front of my daughter once this week. I wasn't going to do it again.

"Don't you have a game to get to?" I asked him. His window was down, and he looked like he was about to speak to me.

"I have about forty-five minutes. Can you talk?"

My response should have been *Nope. I can't. Bye.*

But Brady had a game, and he was here for some

reason. To him, it had to be important. I looked over to see my dad's car was also home. Fridays he often got off work early. The game probably had the entire town getting off work early. Leaving Bryony inside with my parents shouldn't be an issue.

"Let me take her inside," I replied.

I pushed the stroller to the front porch and bent down in front of her to unbuckle the safety harness. "Mommy is going to talk to our friend Brady, okay? I'll be inside to fix you a snack in a few minutes."

She nodded as if this all made sense. I often wondered if it did, if she understood the things she responded to.

Opening the door, I saw Dad on the sofa with a cup of coffee and the newspaper. "Hey, Dad," I greeted him. "Brady Higgens is out here and wants to talk to me a minute. Can you keep an eye on Bryony for me? I won't be long."

Dad frowned. "Brady? Doesn't that boy have a game to be at?"

My sentiments exactly. I nodded. "Yes, so this will be quick."

"Sure, I'll watch her. Tell him I said good luck. I'm rooting for them."

I didn't respond. I wasn't sure what to say. My parents were too enthusiastic about Brady. I was afraid they were about to be let down. I put Bryony down so she could run to see her pops, then closed the door behind me. My father wasn't the nosy sort, but whatever this was about, I didn't want anyone overhearing us.

Brady had stepped out of his truck and was leaning against the passenger's side, waiting on me. I walked back over to him. If he was going to apologize again, I just may have lost my temper. I didn't want his apologies. I wanted to pretend I'd never gone over there.

"I don't have a lot of time," I told him as if he were going to keep me. We both knew he had a game to go win. "And if this is another apology, please don't. Just let it go."

He shifted his feet and seemed almost nervous. "I want to be friends. My original offer—or request—still stands."

What?

"Why?"

He sighed and ran his hands through his messy dark hair. "Because I want to be friends with you. I believe you. I feel like shit about the way I treated you when you first came back into town and the fact that I turned on you two years ago. I was young. That's the only excuse I have. But I know better now. My team doesn't get to tell me who I choose to be friends with."

He sounded so determined I wondered if he was trying

to convince himself of all this. And why he felt the need to come see me before his game when this could wait.

"You've got a championship to win," I reminded him. He'd been pretty set on that the other night.

"Yeah, I do. But that shouldn't stop me from doing what is right."

So I was what was right. That made me feel like a charity case. The kid at the lunch table with no friends. Something he had learned in Sunday school as a kid. *Be kind to those in need.* Well, I wasn't in need. I was perfectly fine.

"I don't need your guilt friendship. I'm better than that. But thanks anyway," I said, then turned to head back inside. This conversation was over as far as I was concerned.

"Wait. Don't. It's not guilt," he called out, but I knew the truth even if he didn't. "The truth is I can't stop thinking about you."

I stopped. Well, that was definitely a turn I hadn't expected.

"Excuse me?" I asked, looking back at him.

He stuck his hands in his jeans pockets. "I think I need you. A friendship that isn't based on my performance on the field or getting into the best party. A real one. That means something."

Now, this was going to be harder to argue or walk away from. I'd been vulnerable at his house the other night, and he was now doing the same with me. It had just taken him time to think it through.

"Why now? Why not when the season is over?"

I can honestly say that I was worried about the other guys and this stupid football game now. Not because I wanted them to win but because I wanted Brady to win. I wanted him to get that future he'd worked so hard for. Why did I want all that? God, I was getting feelings for him. All this crap around us, and I was starting to care about Brady Higgens's happiness.

"Football can't make all my decisions in life for me. If I let it, then I'm not fighting for my dream; I'm letting my dream own me. I should own it."

I stood there in silence and let his words really sink in. He meant this. I respected him for it. But I still wanted to protect him.

"Then let your new friend make a decision for you. Wait. Give this season time to play out. Then we can try the friendship thing."

He shook his head. "I don't want to wait. I can't."

His determination was . . . cute. Admirable but cute.

"Then let's be friends in secret for a few more weeks," I suggested.

He frowned and looked like he was going to argue again.

"Just think about it. Go win tonight's game and let the pros and cons play through your head this weekend. If you're still dead set on blowing up the town, we will go to the Den and eat burgers Monday night. But if you see reason like I do, you'll drive two towns over and meet me for pizza."

A smile slowly spread across his face. "Can I have your number, then?"

As if a female could say no to that.

By Three Touchdowns
CHAPTER 18

BRADY

Getting my head completely in the game was hard, but seeing the fans who had driven out here in the stands, cheering with their banners held high and their cowbells ringing, reminded me of the importance of tonight. I wasn't out here worried about a girl who I couldn't stop thinking about. She was okay now. We were okay. And the idea of a future for us excited rather than scared me. I was ready to win this game now. This wasn't just my future weighing the balance. It was all of ours. Even those of us who would hold this as our last memory of football. It would mean something.

By halftime we were down a touchdown. The Panthers were tough, and even with all the prep work, we were having to be on our very best game to keep up with them. West slung his helmet across the field house as he let out a string of words that I knew Coach would overlook. We hadn't played a game this hard all season.

Gunner slammed his fist into the old, beat-up lockers that were reserved for the Panthers' opposing team. He didn't let a string of curses fly from his mouth, but he continued to beat the locker a few more times before resting his forehead on it. We had two quarters left to change this.

Coach would talk to us and remind us who we were and what we'd come here for. He was good at halftime talks. I could count on him to get the team's heads back up and ready to go fight.

There would be roars and fists in the air as we charged back onto the field. This wasn't the first halftime we had been behind. It was just the first time we had been shaken. The way we had played tonight should have had us a touchdown or more ahead. Not behind.

"Where is your head tonight?" Gunner asked me as he lifted himself up from the locker he'd been leaning on.

Was he blaming me for this? "Not sure what you mean by that," I replied, anger slowly building inside me. The accusation on his face was enough to tell me he was pointing at me instead of all of us. "This is a team. Where is *your* head?" I shot back.

"Fuck that. You've got the ball. You run the team. And I've been playing ball with you since we were kids. Your head isn't with us out there. So where the fucking hell is it? Because we need it on that field." He was yelling now.

"Back off, Gunner," West said, stepping up between us. Nash and Asa had also moved closer to us. As if a fight was about to start and they all needed to be there to break it up.

"No! He is going to lose us this game. His head isn't there, and we need it!" Gunner yelled. "Hunter is a damn sophomore and not ready for this. We can't hand the game over to him. We need Brady to get it together before we walk back onto that field."

I wanted to get in his face and tell him just where he could shove his accusation. The idea of slamming my fist into his face was also appealing. However, he was right. My head wasn't completely there. Gunner was the only one with balls enough to point it out.

"Go drink some water and calm down," Asa told Gunner. They all thought we were about to tie up. Any other time, I just might do it. But tonight Gunner was right. This was my fault. Admitting it hurt, but it was true.

"What's going on out there, boys?" Coach asked as he entered the field house. The local media had stopped him for an interview on his way to us, so he'd missed the confrontation.

Everyone but Gunner turned to look at Coach while Gunner's eyes stayed glued to me. He was waiting on his answer. He wasn't getting one because the truth would cause more than just me messing up. Hell would break loose.

"I'm off tonight," I replied to Coach's question while keeping eye contact with Gunner. "This is all on me."

That was the first moment I'd had to do this in a locker room in all the years I'd been playing. It had never been me. It had always been someone else I had to talk out of whatever funk they were dealing with. This was hard. Like admitting I was a failure.

"Then let's fix this. You're the best senior quarterback in Alabama, Brady. Or did you forget that?" Coach replied.

I hadn't forgotten. I may not agree, but I hadn't forgotten the title had been given to me in the latest stats. If I lost this, Riley would blame herself. This wasn't her fault. It was mine. This wasn't just for me; it was for this entire team and our town.

"I'm ready," I told him.

Coach nodded and started in on his plan for the next half. Now we had seen the Panthers' play and their strategy, we had to adjust ours. I soaked it in and managed to put Riley Young out of my mind. Tonight I had a lot to prove. Especially now.

As we ran back onto the field, Gunner came up beside me. "We've got this."

That was his way of apologizing. Making sure we were okay.

I nodded in agreement. Because we were. We'd win this game tonight. Then we would prepare for next week. It was almost at an end for us and Lion football. Graduation would be our next step.

I was ready for the future, but the smell of the fresh-cut grass and the cheer in the crowd while the guys who learned to play football with me when we were kids were all huddled around me—that would be missed. We'd never get that back.

Because of them, because of that memory and all the others that went with it, I gave everything I had and then some I didn't know I had. With each play called, I focused harder than ever. I drowned out the roar of the fans. I ignored the pop shots called at me from the other team. I had one mission. One drive. To win this game.

And we did. By three touchdowns.

I Owe Tonight to You
CHAPTER 19

RILEY

If I said I went to bed without staying up to watch the news, I would be lying. I was nervous. I had never been nervous over a football game in my entire life. But I was now. I had barely been able to eat dinner, but I had forced myself to so my mother wouldn't question me. Typically I had a great appetite.

Dad was sitting in his recliner with his feet propped up and one of the many blankets my grandmamma had knitted thrown over his legs. His evening bowl of cereal was in his hands as he watched the local news come on. I never watched the news with him, so I tried very casually to walk in and take a seat on the sofa.

Mom was much more observant, so I was thankful tonight she was soaking in a bath at the moment and not out here watching the news with him. She'd question my being out here.

"You still awake?" he asked as if I went to bed early every night. I normally went to my room relatively early, but rarely to sleep. I'd play a game on my phone or read a book. Those sorts of things.

"Yeah," I replied, hoping he left it at that. Normally my dad wasn't a big talker. But when he had something to say, it was always important. He didn't waste words. That's what Mom always said about him.

Thankfully the reporter started talking about gas prices, and Dad fell silent. I could hear him eat the crunchy flakes in his bowl and was glad he had something else to do with his mouth other than talk.

After they covered soaring gas prices, a house burning down in a neighboring town, and the president's new insurance plan, they finally played the clip of a football flying through the air, which meant the local teams' scores were about to be posted.

"The Lawton Lions have done it again" were the first words out of the news anchor's mouth, and I let out an actual sigh of relief. The lady droned on to say that Brady Higgens had struggled through the first half but he'd come back in the second half and owned the game. The Panthers hadn't been ready for him, or at least that was the Panthers' coach's take on it when they asked him. He seemed impressed, and although he was sweating and tired-looking from the game, he agreed that Higgens was the best quarterback in the state. He'd now experienced it and looked forward to following the boy's career.

A little burst of pride welled up in me, and that was silly, but it was the truth. We had been friends as kids but not anything special. I had been friends with all of them. Brady had always been the leader, even when we'd all been playing together on the swing set at the park.

It made sense that he was the leader now. I stood up to leave when the recaps of tonight's game moved on to something else.

"Guess you can sleep now knowing that boy had a good game," Dad said as I was leaving the room.

I paused and winced. I was a little obvious walking out just after that news. "He was nervous and possibly the only friend I'll ever have in this town."

That was the best explanation I had, and it was the truth.

"He's a good kid. Talented athlete. But I will say I'm more proud of him for ignoring the rest of them and reaching out to be your friend anyway. He has a lot riding on him, so to see him take a stand like this gives me hope for that bunch after all. Brady is their leader. They may buck him at first but eventually . . ." He trailed off.

I wasn't going to think that way, nor would I get my hopes up. Brady couldn't take away all the hate that was set in from what happened with Rhett. I often wondered, would this all have been better if I had just left town and not told anyone? I would never know the answer to that, and figured that was okay. I didn't need to know. My life had turned out the way it was supposed to. I was a firm believer in fate. So far fate had given me Bryony and I couldn't complain. She was perfect. My perfect.

"Good night, Dad," I said before leaving this time.

"Good night, sweetheart."

I went down the hall and slowly eased the bedroom door open so I wouldn't wake my sleeping princess. She was curled up into a ball with most of the covers, and I loved watching her like this. She was safe and secure in the life I'd given her. She knew nothing about how she was conceived or the pain that had followed it. There was no need for her to know.

Bending down, I kissed the top of her head, and the sweet smell of baby shampoo met my nose. I loved smelling her. The house had smelled like this—baby—when I had brought her home from the hospital. That smell reminded me of sleepless nights but also of first smiles, first kisses, first words, and first steps. I loved everything about that smell. I often wondered if I could convince her to keep using the same shampoo into her teen years. I doubted it, but there was always hope.

My phone was sitting on the nightstand. Although it was on silent, the screen lit up the room. I never got texts or calls unless they were from my parents. The only person who had my number now was on a bus celebrating a victory.

I hurried around the bed and picked it up.

Brady's name appeared, so I swiped my finger over the screen and read his words.

Thank you. I owe tonight to you.

That wasn't true. He owed tonight to the fact that he was a star. I had nothing to do with it.

I seriously doubt that, but congratulations, I replied.

He would be leaving town this summer. Going off to live his dreams. And I would be here with my parents until I could get a place of my own in a town where I could start over and have a life.

If you hadn't talked to me today, I wouldn't have been able to concentrate, he replied.

Had my going over to his house really bothered him that much? I wanted to let the flutters in my stomach fly free and enjoy this, but I couldn't. I wasn't a girl in high school who could flirt and have fun. I was a mom and a daughter with responsibilities. I lived a life he didn't understand and I didn't expect him to fit into.

"Enjoy your win. I watched the news. You deserved it."

I didn't wait for him to reply. I turned my phone over and laid it down. Young girls' fantasies were not for me.

Fun Game Last Night, Huh?

CHAPTER 20

BRADY

Saturdays after a game I should sleep in. However, sleep didn't come easily last night, and the smell of bacon woke me up earlier than I'd have liked. I reached for my phone and checked to see if Riley ever responded to my last text. She didn't.

Jerking on a pair of sweats, I headed downstairs to the kitchen for breakfast. My mom was piling up a stack of pancakes with her pink-and-white apron tied around her waist. I had bought it for her five years ago for Mother's Day with money I'd made mowing grass. She wore it all the time.

"Morning," I said as I headed over to the fridge to get the milk.

"You're up early. I expected you to sleep until noon," she teased.

I hadn't slept until noon, well . . . ever. She knew better. "I smelled the bacon," I told her. "A man can't sleep when there is bacon."

That got a laugh from her.

Mom had always been that mom. The one who made our lunches and cooked us breakfast. The mom who made cookies and let me have a den full of guys over. She believed in me and was proud of me. In return I wanted to continue to make her proud. I had been given a mom most guys weren't lucky enough to have. At least not in my group of friends. I was lucky that way. Not a lot of moms were as perfect as mine. For example, Gunner's mom. I wasn't even sure she deserved that title. She hadn't done much for him in life.

"You sore from last night?" Mom asked as she placed a plate of pancakes and bacon on the table for me.

I had a few sensitive spots but nothing worth mentioning. Those were from some ringers in the first half that I deserved. My head hadn't been where it needed to be. "I'm good," I assured her.

She smiled at me, then went back to the pancakes. "I saw the hits you took in the second quarter. You're bound to have a few bad spots."

I shrugged and reached for the syrup to coat my pancakes in. "Dad still in bed?" I asked, changing the subject.

"No, you know your dad. He got up early and headed to the office. Said he needed to get caught up on things, and he'd see us at dinner. I'm sure he'll be ready to talk football by then."

My dad always had to be doing something. He worked a lot, and being idle wasn't even in his vocabulary. He was funny like that.

I started to make a joke about it when my phone screen lit up. I grabbed it and saw Riley's name. I glanced back to make sure Mom wasn't looking my way before opening the text. Not that she would disapprove. I knew she liked Riley. Mom was the least judgmental person I knew. But I didn't want my parents to know yet. Not about my friendship with Riley. I was still holding that close. Just for me.

Sure, if you need someone to ride with you to Birmingham today, I will. Mom said she could watch Bryony. Why are we going?

I had just thrown that out there. A two-hour drive to Birmingham had been the only thing I could think of. It was far enough away from Lawton that we could safely enjoy ourselves without running into someone we knew. I hadn't thought of a reason why I needed to go. I'd just said I did. Now I needed something. Any excuse so she didn't know I was simply going there so we could hang out. Alone.

And why was I doing that?

She needed a friend, and I wanted to be her friend, but there was more to it than all that. Last night, when I was distracted, I wanted to believe it was because I was worried about her or something that innocent. But the truth was, I liked her.

I liked Riley Young. She was interesting. She was strong, She was a good person, and I respected her for all of that. I wanted to be around her. Away from the same group of people I was always around. Maybe that was why I had liked Willa. She was different. Not the same crowd doing the same things.

I liked her even though my being her friend was going to cause a stir eventually. The confrontation with Gunner was the one I dreaded the most. But honestly, it was time he faced the fact that his brother had lied. After all they had been through lately, I didn't think it was going to be too big of a stretch for him to believe Riley's story now. We weren't kids who let others tell us what to think anymore.

I finally replied. I have some birthday money still in my savings account, and I wanted a pair of boots that are sold out here. Birmingham has better options.

I doubted that sounded believable since Nashville was only an hour away. But I went with it anyway.

"It smells wonderful in this house," Maggie said,

walking into the kitchen. Her hair was still messy from sleep, and she was wearing a pair of pajama pants and one of West's shirts. He had made sure she had several of them. It was his way of being with her all the time. I used to make fun of that, but now I thought it made sense. Not that I'd tell him that. I liked the idea of Riley wearing my shirt. Which also meant my feelings for her were changing into something more than friendship.

"Have a seat and I'll get you a plate," Mom told her.

Maggie ignored that and walked over to pick up her own plate. "You're still cooking. I can fix my own plate. Thank you, though."

Mom smiled as if Maggie were the perfect daughter she never had. They were good for each other. Mom was the kind of mom who needed a daughter, and Maggie had lost her mother tragically. They weren't as close as a mother and daughter could get, but I expected over time they would fill that hole in each other's lives.

Maggie sat down across from me and yawned. Just a couple months ago this would have been a very silent table. It was nice that Maggie actually spoke now. "Fun game last night, huh?"

Her comment sounded innocent, but I knew what she meant. She was the only person who had an idea of where my head had been that first half. I looked up at her as I put a bite of pancake in my mouth. I wasn't amused. But the smirk on her face said she was.

"It about gave me a heart attack," Mom said with a chuckle. "Lord, I've never been so nervous over a game in all my life."

"The games are going to just get harder. Winning the championship isn't meant to be easy." I realized I sounded annoyed and wished I hadn't said that.

Maggie raised one eyebrow as if to say she knew better. Why couldn't she just have stayed upstairs in bed? I was having a perfectly peaceful breakfast until she came in and brought this all up.

"Oh, I know. I realized last night I needed to calm down and prepare for this to just get worse." Mom's voice was still gentle and understanding.

"I'm sure it's hard to keep your focus with all that pressure," Maggie added, then grinned before eating a piece of bacon.

I was either going to stop eating and leave the table with an excuse or change the subject. But I wasn't full and I wanted more pancakes, so I went with the subject change. "Want me to take Dad some breakfast before I head to Birmingham?" I asked.

Maggie snickered. I was about to throw my last pancake at her amused face.

She's My Spot of
Sunshine in Life
CHAPTER 21

RILEY

My parents hadn't really questioned Brady picking me up to go to Birmingham for the day. I gave them the reason why Brady needed to go, but neither looked as if they believed it. I wondered myself if that was really the reason. I figured Nashville had just as good shopping as Birmingham. I could assume that he had found a pair in Birmingham. However, the idea that he was making up this excuse to spend the day with me made my heart do funny things. I liked it. Again I was feeling too much, and I really needed to be more cautious.

I didn't let Dad talk too long to Brady when he arrived. He of course told him good game and said he wished he'd seen it. I had pushed him out the door and escaped before Dad could say too much else. I never knew what was going to come out of his mouth.

Brady's truck wasn't what I assumed a teenage guy's truck to be like inside. For starters, it was clean. No trash on the floorboard, it didn't stink like a locker room, and it wasn't even dusty on the dash. He kept it really nice.

"Do you get your truck detailed often?" I asked as I looked around at the cleanliness for the first time. The last two times I was in this truck I was preoccupied and hadn't really paid attention.

"My dad would take this truck away from me if I paid someone to clean it," Brady said, sounding amused. "He'd also take it away from me if I didn't keep it spotless."

Interesting. He was the football star, but that didn't give him special treatment from his parents. I would have thought otherwise. Especially in this town. I imagined he had people begging to clean his truck for free.

"Sounds like my dad. He expects me to do my part. Not that I wouldn't anyway, but I know if I slack off he is there to remind me to get my ass in gear."

Brady chuckled. "Yeah. I know that feeling."

We were quiet then for a few minutes. I didn't feel the need to talk just to make conversation. There were plenty of things I could ask him. Like why were we really going to Birmingham? But for now I wasn't doing that. I'd enjoy the ride and being out of the house with someone my age. It had been two years since I'd done anything like this.

It made me feel older than I was. Brady didn't make me feel old, though. He wasn't blaring music and talking about himself. That was how I remembered guys my age. But then I wasn't used to the way they aged. My only experience was watching television shows and movies. This was much more pleasant than I had expected.

I didn't want to enjoy it too much because the fact that this could all end abruptly was there. Hanging in the distance. When it came down to it, I didn't expect Brady to choose me over Gunner. And that would be the outcome when Gunner found out. Our town was small, and for a couple weeks we could keep our friendship hidden, but it would come out. Brady was being optimistic. He believed it would all work out.

I'd lived through hell. I knew how it all ended. Hopefulness and optimism were things I'd grown out of.

"When is the last time you've been to Birmingham?" he asked.

Good question. I wasn't sure. "Years, I guess. I can't even remember."

"Did you go to school when you moved away?"

I shook my head and stared out the window. "No. After

leaving, I wasn't brave enough to face more teenagers and their judgment about my pregnancy. I began homeschooling then."

He didn't respond right away, and I wished we hadn't gotten on this topic. It was awkward for him, I guess. And not something I liked to talk about.

"Wasn't that lonely?"

He had no idea. "Yeah, but then Bryony was born and she changed my world."

That was the truth. Before her birth I had been depressed. My world was lost, and I didn't think I'd ever smile again. Being fifteen and pregnant was terrifying. Even if you had the support of your parents.

"You're a good mom. You make it look easy, even though I know it can't be."

Bryony made it easy. She was such a good baby. It was almost like she was born knowing I needed easy. The moment they laid her on my chest I started to cry. Not because I was scared or sad but because she was mine. Perfect, beautiful, and healthy. I'd brought a life into this world, and nothing I ever did after that would be as important.

"She's my spot of sunshine in life," I replied. She was worth every teenage moment lost. I wouldn't trade her to get any of it back. I would never suggest being a teen mom to someone, because it wasn't a life choice. But when there is no option and it's placed upon you, you then learn to survive and make the best of it. Bryony was definitely the best.

"Are you going to just graduate from your online homeschooling courses? Or have you considered going back to school?"

I never considered it. Nor could I. "I have responsibilities that won't change. My parents need my help with my grandmother, and then there is Bryony. I don't want her in a day care. She needs me."

"I wonder if any of the girls at school would think the same way you do. Somehow I doubt it," he replied. "I respect that."

I wasn't really after his respect, but I didn't say that. I did this for my family because I loved them. Not to get a pat on the back.

"So tell me about these boots and why you need them this badly," I said, changing the subject off me.

Finally turning my attention from the road to my right, I looked over at him. He had a small grin on his face. "They're just some I want."

"Okay . . . well, you can't order them online or go to Nashville to find them?"

His grin got a little bigger. "I could. But then I wouldn't

have a reason to get you far enough away from Lawton so we could enjoy ourselves for the day."

"Are you saying this trip is so we can hang out?" I asked, my heart doing that silly little squeeze and flutter.

He glanced over at me. "Yeah. I guess it is."

I didn't ask any more. That was enough. Enough to make me forget this was going to end too. Most good things did.

CHAPTER 22

BRADY

Our conversation became easy, and the two hours didn't seem that long at all. When Riley laughed, I wanted to soak it in. The sound of it was . . . nice. No, it was more than nice. I craved it. I found myself trying to coax a laugh from her. Anything to hear her and watch her face light up.

I received a few texts, and each one I ignored. Gunner's, West's, and Asa's had been expected. The one from Ivy hadn't, but I ignore hers normally anyway. Today I wasn't living in that world. I was living in the world I chose to live in.

"I've never had barbecue this good," Riley said as she

wiped her mouth with a napkin. I couldn't think of one girl I'd ever dated that would have chosen a barbecue place to eat and then ordered ribs covered in sauce. Most of them ate things that weren't messy. But Riley was enjoying her food. Getting sauce all over her hands and face didn't bother her at all.

Seeing her laugh at the mess she was making was cute. I wanted to sit here all day and experience this. I picked up another hot wing and cleaned the bone. Normally I was a cleaner eater because my date was. But with Riley I felt like I could eat as if she were one of the guys. Although she looked nothing like one of the guys.

If girls realized how attractive it was to be so free and happy about something as simple as some ribs, they'd lighten up a bit. The guys two tables over from us kept checking Riley out, and although it was annoying that they didn't seem to mind that she was with me, I couldn't actually blame them.

I was having a hard time taking my eyes off her too.

"I'm going to have to go wash my face in the bathroom after this," she said with a smile. "Bryony loves ribs. I wish she were here for these."

I'd offer to take some back with us, but they'd be bad by the time we finished our day and drove the two hours back.

"I could grill some for her sometime. Y'all could come over for dinner."

Riley paused for a moment and a mix of emotions flashed in her eyes. She put a rib down and let out a small sigh. "Yeah, maybe."

What was that about? She seemed almost upset by my offer, or disappointed.

"Did I say something wrong?"

She was looking down at her ribs then lifted her eyes to mine. "I don't live in a fantasy world, Brady. I've had too much reality for that. Truth is, when your friends find out that you're spending time with me, it will stop. Because you'll have to choose. They'll make you. And I don't expect you to choose me."

What the hell did that mean? I wasn't going to have to choose anyone. I was my own man, dammit, and if I wanted to pick my friends, I could. I didn't need anyone's permission.

"I'm not like that. I'd have hoped you knew that already. No one makes me do anything."

She shrugged and cleaned her hands off on a napkin. "It's not a bad thing. It just is what it is. Here we have no judgment, and I enjoy being with you. I like this. Having a friend. But I'm not delusional. I know everyone in Lawton hates me and thinks I'm a liar. Well, everyone but you."

I had never been openly hated. I wondered what that felt like. How painful and unfair it must be. My anger rose up at all of them. Everyone who had talked bad about her. Everyone who had judged her or been cruel to her. Then I admitted to myself the hardest part: I was one of those everyones. Maybe not now, but I had been once. I wasn't any better.

"I'm sorry," I said honestly.

She smiled. "For being my friend?"

"No. For turning on you when I did."

The smile on her face faded. "We were young. You thought what everyone else did. Besides, I ran out of town. It made me look even more guilty. If I had stayed, life for my family would have just gotten worse, but the fact is we left. People feel sorry for my parents because of me. But these people'll always hate me. The good thing is I won't always be there. I'll get out and make my own way in life soon enough. In a town where no one knows me and I can start fresh. Me and Bryony."

The image of Riley taking Bryony to some town far away and building a life, getting a job, paying bills, raising her daughter, all while I was off throwing a football and chasing my dream, seemed unfair. So much of her life seemed unfair. She'd missed high school and she'd miss college.

"What was your dream, when you were younger?" I asked her. I didn't want to say *before Bryony*, because that sounded cold. Although that was what I wanted to know.

"You mean before I became a mom?" She was smiling as if she read my mind. "I wanted to be a vet."

"So you love animals," I said, feeling my heart ache for the girl who wouldn't be able to chase her dream the way I would.

"Yes. I do. I can't take care of one now because I can't afford it. But when Bryony and I have our own place, we will have dogs and cats. Maybe even goats if I get enough land."

"Could you still go to college to be a vet?"

She shook her head. "No, I need a job that makes enough to support me and Bryony. I have plans. I want to make a difference in girls' lives like me one day. The teen mom support group I went to got me through tough times. My dream is to do that for young girls. Show them there is happiness in their future. Life isn't over."

She didn't say it with bitterness or anger. Instead she took a drink of her sweet tea and stood up. "I need to go wash myself off," she explained before walking to the back of the restaurant to the restrooms.

Why did I want her to have that dream so badly? She seemed happy enough, and I had never wanted to fix anyone's problems as much as I wanted to fix hers. She made me want to protect her and stand by her. Even though she may have been one of the toughest people I'd ever met. If she knew what I was thinking, she'd tell me to stop. She had everything under control.

Maybe that was why I wanted to help her so much. Because she didn't want help. She wanted to make her own way. And I knew she could.

"Hey, y'all just friends or is she with you?" one of the guys asked from the other table.

I turned to look at him, and his obvious interest pissed me off. Sure, I understood it, but I was jealous. Me. Jealous. Not the kind I felt with Gunner and Willa, but the kind that made me want to stake my claim and threaten him.

"She's with me," I replied in a cold tone.

The guy looked let down. "Damn" was his response.

*I Didn't Know Friends
Kissed Like That*

CHAPTER 23

RILEY

It was after six when Brady pulled into my driveway. I had
kept in contact with my mom all day, and Bryony had been
fine. As much as I missed her, this little getaway had been
needed. I was thankful Brady had thought of it.

I turned to tell him thank you and how much I enjoyed
our day when he pulled to a stop, but his gaze was already
locked on me. The look in his eyes was different, and I recognized it. Or at least my body did. My heart had picked
up its pace, and I felt flushed from anticipation.

Before I could get too nervous or think this through, he
leaned over and his right hand cupped my cheek just as he
leaned his head down until his lips touched mine. It wasn't

controlling or possessive. It wasn't like a hungry teenage boy trying to attack me. It was sweet. Like he wanted to savor this.

I moved my body closer to his and opened my mouth beneath his, hoping that wasn't too much too soon. Although this was not how I expected this day to end. Not that deep down I hadn't wanted it. Because I had. I knew that. It was just actually having it happen was different. It was exciting and terrifying. Reality had been much different in my head. I had even been debating giving him a hug earlier, not realizing he was planning on this.

His tongue touched mine, and I let out a sound that I hoped sounded as pleased as I was. A real kiss. The kind that meant something was new to me. What I had done before when I was younger had been learning and experimenting. Nothing more. It sure hadn't made my heart flutter and my body tingle.

I wanted to remember this in case our end came sooner than expected. Although Brady wasn't my first kiss, he would always be my first meaningful kiss. The first one to affect me.

Slowly he eased back, ending the connection.

"I've wanted to do that all day," he whispered.

I hadn't realized it, but I was blushing from his admission and thankful for the darkness.

"I didn't know friends kissed like that," I replied.

He pressed a small kiss to the corner of my lips. "They don't" was his response.

"Oh" was all I could say. Brady was telling me this was more. It wasn't just me feeling things beyond friendship. He was feeling them too.

"Can I call you tomorrow?" he asked, sounding unsure.

I wondered if Brady Higgens had ever been unsure about anything. "Yes."

He moved away and climbed down out of his truck. I watched him as he walked around the front of his truck and came to open my door. He held out his hand to help me down, and I took it. Not because I needed it but because I wasn't sure how well my legs were going to work now.

"Thanks for today," I said, wanting to say more but so flustered I couldn't seem to find the words.

"It was the best day I've had in a long time," he replied.

I knew he wouldn't kiss me out here. For the world to see. Even now, him walking me to my door was dangerous. If anyone drove by and saw him, he'd have to lie or tell the truth. I wanted him to lie. I wasn't ready for this to end. Not yet.

"We will find some time tomorrow, then," he said just as we reached the door.

I knew I couldn't leave Bryony all day again, and

I didn't want to. "Yeah, I can get away for a little while. Maybe while Bryony naps."

"Soon we can take her to the park together."

I liked that he said that, but believing him was hard, so I just nodded.

"Good night," he said reaching down to squeeze my hand before turning and leaving me there.

I opened the front door and stepped inside, even though I wanted to watch him until he drove away. I wouldn't allow myself that.

"That looked like your day went well," my mother said with her eyebrows up as I walked into the living room. She'd been spying on me. I hadn't expected her to do that.

"I don't know what you mean," I replied, blowing that off.

She rolled her eyes. "It may be dark outside, but under the streetlamp the inside of his truck was perfectly clear from here. Don't get me wrong—I wasn't spying. I just heard his truck and decided to check to see who was here. Then I saw something I wasn't expecting."

Me either.

"Don't read too much into it," I replied.

"Momma!" Bryony called out, running excitedly into the room with her bath towel wrapped around her.

"Hey, baby girl," I said, equally as thrilled to see her.

"Baff!" she stated the obvious.

"Then I'll go bathe you," I replied.

"Pay boat." She loved her little pink boat that floated in the bathwater. Playing boat was her favorite part of her bath.

"Okay, sounds like a plan."

"Ookies," she said, pointing to the kitchen.

She nodded enthusiastically.

"He likes you. Trust him," Mother called out as I followed my daughter down the hall.

"I'm trying" was my only response. "But I know how this ends."

"You don't know him. That boy is different. He always has been."

I remembered him turning on me two years ago. He wasn't different then. "He's nicer, but in the end he isn't all that different."

I could hear my mother's sigh, and I kept following Bryony to the bathroom. Spending time with my daughter and reminding myself what was important in life was what I needed after that kiss. I wasn't a normal girl, and sitting around and dwelling on it was pointless.

"One day you're going to have to trust again," Mom replied, following us to the bathroom. She wasn't ready to let this go.

One day I was. Today wasn't that day.

"Did you save me some cookies?" I asked her.

"Of course. Bryony made you pink ones."

I had heard her, but I wanted a subject change. That had worked.

"What all did you do today?" I asked Bryony.

"Ookies," she told me again.

Cooking anything was the highlight of her day, other than going to the park. Especially cooking things she liked to eat.

"Did you play outside?"

She nodded. "Me duddy." She beamed up at me as if being dirty was an accomplishment.

"Then you had a perfect day," I reminded her.

She dropped her towel and ran to the bathwater that my mother had run for her. It was full of her toys and bubbles.

This was my enough.

CHAPTER 24

BRADY

West had woken me up at nine this morning. He was going for a run and wanted me to go with him. Maggie had turned him down, so I got up and went. It was good to work out the stiffness from Friday night. It also gave Mom time to fix breakfast.

The route he was taking us on went right in front of Riley's house. My plan had been to text her this morning and find some way to see her. I'd lain in bed for hours last night thinking about our day. Her laughter, her smile, the feel of her lips on mine. All of it. I wanted to see her again. Now.

Looking toward the house, I wondered if she was

awake and what she was doing. Did Bryony wake her up early? Did she fix breakfast at her house? Was her grandmother being difficult today? What did she normally do on Sundays? I had a million questions. I wanted to know everything about her. I just needed time and freedom to run up to her door right now and see her.

"What's going on there?" West asked, and it snapped my attention back to the road we were on and the fact that I wasn't alone.

"What do you mean?" was my response. Although I knew exactly what he meant.

"With Riley," he replied.

West wouldn't be on Maggie's side about this. Sure, he'd offered to help find her grandmother, but he wasn't about to become her friend.

"They're living here taking care of her grandmother," I told him, although I knew he already knew that.

"Not what I meant, and you know it."

I didn't say anything to that. We were running, not talking. He needed to stop being nosy and focus on his own love life. Mine was off-limits.

"You suck at hiding things. It's going to come out," he finally said when I didn't say anything.

"Nothing to hide," I lied.

He laughed. "Sure."

I picked up speed in hopes of getting home and safe from his questioning faster.

"Gunner's gonna find out. Then all hell will break loose. Might as well tell me now what you're thinking. You're my best friend. I'm not going to turn on you."

Out of everyone, I never really expected West to turn on me. He was closer to me than he was Gunner. There was also Maggie, who was going to take my side in this. And there was no way West wouldn't be on Maggie's side.

"Right now there isn't anything to find out. After we win the championship, then things may change." That was all he was getting out of me.

"You need to do a better job of hiding it, then. Because at this rate you're gonna get found out and you'll have Gunner to deal with. We need him to win."

He'd have his followers too. People who would side with him and turn on me. That would split the team, and we would be over. I had played this scenario in my head a million times, it seemed. I knew how it went and how it ended.

"I've got this under control," I assured him.

"The way you were looking at her house, it didn't seem like it."

Point made. I had to back off for now. I could talk to Riley on the phone and see her when we could get out of town on weekends. Just for the next two weeks. Then I'd be free.

"Noted," I replied. Luckily my house was in sight and this conversation could be over.

We ran up to the sidewalk in silence and slowed as we got to the door. Just before my hand touched the knob to go inside, West said one more thing. "Even if Rhett didn't do it, she was still only fifteen. He shouldn't have been alone with her."

I paused. I knew Rhett had done it. But he was right. Even if he hadn't, the situation was still bad. Rhett had no business with her, and everyone knew he was sleeping with other girls in our grade. Serena, to be exact. It wasn't like he was above it.

"Yeah. I know. But he did it" was all I said before going inside to the smell of biscuits and sausage.

"Your house always smells like food. I love it here," West said as we walked to the kitchen.

"That's because you only come at mealtimes."

"When it's not a mealtime, it smells like cookies."

I laughed as we entered the kitchen to find Mom in her apron and Maggie putting butter in biscuits. She glanced up and made eye contact with West before smiling.

"Smells good, Mom," I told her, ignoring the lovebirds and going to the fridge to get the milk.

"You two stink," she replied. "Have a good run?"

"Woke me up," I said.

West chuckled and sat down. I didn't look his way, but I could feel Maggie studying the two of us. She was good with body language and would have this figured out soon enough.

"Ivy came by yesterday. I forgot to tell you when you got home last night. She left you some cinnamon rolls. I put them in the fridge."

My mom knew my issues with Ivy, but she reminded me to be kind to her. The girl was hard to shake when you were kind, though.

"She needs to stop that," I said with an annoyed grunt.

"I like the brownies," Maggie replied, sounding amused.

"Well, you can have them," I told her.

"You gonna share with me?" West asked.

"Of course. I can't eat them all."

I rolled my eyes at their attempt at humor and fixed my plate before my mom could. "Thanks for cooking," I told her, then sat down to get full after burning all those calories.

"Do you think she'd send some of that caramel pound cake her mom makes?" West teased.

I ignored him.

"Wouldn't hurt to ask," Maggie added.

"All right, you two, stop giving Brady a hard time," Mom said with a smile in her voice. She patted me on the back.

I doubted Riley would ever send me food, and I was good with that.

CHAPTER 25

RILEY

It was after lunch when my phone rang. I was just about to take Bryony to the park. Brady's name lit up the screen and a smile crossed my face. Just seeing his name made me smile. I was getting too into him. This could end badly, and I could be hurt.

"Hello," I said, stepping outside away from my family's ears.

"Hey, what are you up to today?"

"Well, Bryony and I had a picnic in the backyard and now we are getting ready for our outing to the park. I also need to pick Mom up some milk and eggs at the grocery store."

Talking about my daily routine with him was a little awkward. As casual as I tried to make all that sound, it felt as if I was describing something so foreign to him he wouldn't get it.

"Sounds like a full day. Not too cold for a picnic with the sun out, I guess," he replied. It was the kind of response one made when they didn't know what else to say. He understood nothing of having a kid to take care of.

"What have you been up to?" I asked, trying to change the subject to something else.

"West woke me up to run this morning, then we ate breakfast and watched the game video from Friday night." He didn't tell me what he was going to do next. Not that it was my business.

"I haven't been running in the morning in two years," I replied, remembering when I had once been on the track team. I'd enjoyed it. Part of me missed it.

"Maybe one morning next weekend you could go with me. That is, if your parents could watch Bryony."

He wasn't thinking about the fact that we'd be seen. He forgot that often. "We might need to wait a couple weeks. When we aren't hiding the friendship thing."

He was silent a moment. I always wondered what he was thinking when he did that.

"Is that what we are?"

What kind of question was that?

"I'm not sure I follow you," I replied.

"Friends."

Oh. We'd kissed. Had that changed everything? Did kissing make it different? I was rusty with the dating thing. Guys confused me in general.

"I'm not sure we can ever be more," I said. Had he forgotten the biggest barrier that stood between us?

"Why?"

Apparently he *had* forgotten. So I stated the obvious. "I'm a teenage mom and you leave in six months to live your dream at the college of your choice. Anything more would end anyway. Friends is the safest thing for us." Or for me. Because when he left, I'd be the one struggling to make life work. He would never know any of that.

"Can we say for now that we will work things out as they come? Because I'd like more of last night. And the day we spent together was the best time I've had in a long time."

My face flushed and my heart fluttered. Brady Higgens liked me. He wanted to see more of me, and he wanted more kissing. I agreed with all of that. The problem was he'd only gotten a taste of me. Just me. Not Bryony, and the two of us were a package deal. She'd always come first.

"Maybe you should give it time before you decide that.

You've never dated a teenage mom before, I'd be safe to assume."

He didn't reply right away, so I gave him time to process. Brady's life was one of fairy tales. Actual real-life issues didn't register easily with him. I'd once been the same way. So I understood it.

"Give me a chance to prove to you this could be different."

That was Brady living in his fairy-tale land. Being around him made me miss that. The not expecting anything bad to happen. But I had been weak then. I wasn't now. Life had made me tough.

"Let's just take it a day at a time. No promises. No plans. Just live it." If I didn't do this, I would regret it. Possibly forever. Brady was different, and being with him made me happy. I wanted more of how he made me feel. The future was going to hurt, but for now, I would enjoy it.

He sighed and I smiled. This wasn't what he was used to. Getting what he wanted was easy. I wasn't being easy. Maybe I'd toughen him up a bit.

"I'll take whatever you're offering," he replied. He sounded let down that I hadn't promised him the moon. He was used to the moon. He was used to girls chasing him, like Ivy did. I'd seen that just watching from my quiet life, unattached to everyone. Until a few weeks ago, Ivy was always with Brady. I wasn't exactly sure what had ended that, but he seemed ready to move on.

"Bryony is ready for the park. I need to go," I told him. It was a reminder to both of us that I had priorities.

"Yeah, okay. Anyway, you think you could get out tonight?"

Asking my parents to watch Bryony again was too much. I never did that. "I put her to bed at eight thirty. After she's asleep I could ask my parents to listen out for her."

"I'll be there at nine," he replied.

After we hung up I didn't think too much about it. Because I would only remind myself how much of an impossibility a future with us was. He was a right-now friend. Or he was supposed to be. The kiss had definitely changed things.

"Park!" Bryony demanded, pulling on my shorts leg.

"Yes, it's time for the park," I agreed.

She clapped and hurried down the hall toward the front door.

"We are headed to the park," I called out to my parents, who were in the kitchen.

"All right, y'all have fun," Mom replied.

"Have you seen Thomas?" Grandmamma asked, walking into the living room behind me.

"No, not today," I replied. *Or ever*, I thought to myself.

She frowned. "He's taken my slippers. He likes my slippers."

"Which ones?" I asked, thinking maybe I could find them.

"The pink fuzzy bunny ones. He took those."

Grandmamma didn't own a pair of pink bunny slippers. At least not in this decade. Or the past six. This was another item she remembered from her childhood. She had asked about them before, and Mom had been here to explain. I didn't argue, though. "I'll keep my eyes open for them."

"And Thomas. Look for Thomas. He needs to eat."

"Yes, ma'am," I replied. "I'll do that."

*I Would Never Be
That Guy Again*

CHAPTER 26

BRADY

I was going to take Dad's truck tonight. It was the best way not to feel as if we had to sneak around. No one would be looking for me in Dad's truck. My truck, however, would draw attention. Mom said Dad had gone into the office today to do some work, so I headed that way after my conversation with Riley. She needed proof I was serious, and I understood that she wasn't like the other girls I knew. She was a mom. It was her differences that drew me to her. She didn't bore me. She was real.

Getting her to trust me, however, was something else I needed to prepare for. It wasn't going to be easy. She was very closed off and careful. I hadn't been able to think about anything but her after our day yesterday, but she seemed unaffected. Completely. That wasn't something I knew how to handle.

I pulled up outside Dad's office building and grabbed my phone off the passenger seat and tucked it in my pocket before getting out of the truck. Explaining that I needed to borrow his truck and why was going to be awkward. I wasn't sure if he was okay with Riley, if he believed Rhett like everyone else in town or if he thought she might have told the truth. I also knew he didn't want me distracted from football.

If he saw Riley as a distraction, then we may have an argument. Either way he was going to have to come to terms with this and be okay. I never asked him for his opinion on things like this, and I wasn't about to start. I loved him, but this was my life. My choices.

The front door was unlocked, and I headed inside and toward the back of the building, where I knew his office was. No other cars were outside, so when I heard voices I slowed down. He could be in a meeting, and I didn't want to interrupt him. I could wait until it was over.

The female sound that drifted down the hall caused me to freeze. Not just my body but my breathing. I think even my heart stopped. The next sound that followed was an obvious moan and then my dad's deep voice making a sound that he should not be making in his office.

I had to be mistaken. That wasn't my dad. He wouldn't do that.

Forcing my feet to walk forward I went toward the sound, toward the office I knew was Dad's, and with each step their sounds became louder and more intense. My stomach turned, and I wasn't sure if I was going to throw up before I even got there. Every word and sound he made just proved me wrong. It was him. Who else could it be?

There was a mirror behind my dad's desk that my mother had hung when she decorated his office. This very same mirror now showed my father clearly undressed. A woman with long blond hair sat on his desk, and he was between her legs. Moving. The red heels on her feet sickened me, and the cry of his name from her lips made me so ill I had to turn and run. I was going to be sick.

This wasn't happening. Not my dad. He had my mom. Why would he do that to her? With a woman half his age? I hadn't seen her face clearly over his shoulder, but she was definitely younger.

Never had my heart shattered like it had just now. Not once in my life had I really felt pain like this. I thought I'd understood what it was like to be hurt. But I realized as I exited that building and the cool air hit my face that *this* was what real pain felt like. It tore you open. Burned you. Destroyed everything you were and left you bent over in a parking lot, heaving until there was nothing left in your stomach.

I stayed like that, bent over, until I was sure that was all I had in me. Standing back up, my body felt weak, empty, lost. I'd left my house thirty minutes ago completely at ease. And in one moment it had all changed. I would never be that guy again.

As I looked at my dad's truck, hate, anger, and disbelief all slammed into my chest. I wanted to go inside and tell him what a worthless piece of shit he was. That I hoped he rotted in hell for this. I wanted to throw rocks at his truck windows and take a key down the side of the paint. I wanted him as destroyed as I was.

Picturing my mother's face stopped me, and I sank down into my seat and laid my head on the steering wheel. This would kill her. She adored that man. She did everything for him. If she found out, she'd be so crushed, and I wasn't sure she could make it. I loved her, but she wasn't that strong.

Starting my truck, I headed for home then stopped. I couldn't face her. Not now. I couldn't face anyone. I needed to be alone. So I turned my truck north and drove. It was all I could do: drive away from the false sense of security I had lived in here.

Football no longer seemed important. College no longer weighed on my mind. Just the fact that my family was living a lie and my father was about to completely destroy all I'd known. I would never forgive him. I couldn't bleach my brain and unsee that. If I could, I would.

We had everything. *He* had everything, and he was throwing it away for what? Some woman who looked hot in a miniskirt?

Asa passed me and honked, but I couldn't even wave back. I didn't want to. That was my past life. The one where I wanted to make my dad proud. The one where I cared about my future. The one where my mother was loved and provided for. Everyone in this town was a part of that life.

Were they all living a lie? Was no one real? Was life here one big fat production?

I drove looking straight ahead, my head pounding from the powerful vomiting and the sight that wouldn't go away replaying in my head. Stopping meant I'd have to go back there. I never wanted to go back there. I never wanted to see that man again.

He had ruined it all. For me. For my mom. For the football team. For this town.

Because Brady Higgens was broken. I wouldn't work properly now. I just didn't give a fuck. I'd done my best to be the kid everyone was proud of. I'd played by the rules and I'd been good.

What good had that done me? None whatsoever. My dad was a fucking whore.

The Fairy Tale from Our Childhood Is Gone

CHAPTER 27

RILEY

It was almost eleven when I put my phone down and climbed into bed. Brady hadn't called, and he hadn't come by at nine like he said. I could have texted him, but I had too much pride for that. He was the one who had asked to meet up with me tonight. I hadn't asked him.

The idea that something could be wrong with him played in my head. I finally pushed it away. If he'd been hurt, I would know by now. The entire town would know. I forced my eyes closed and listened to Bryony's even breathing. She was here, and that was all that I needed.

Trusting a guy, even one like Brady, was stupid. They were all the same. He had a better option come open tonight and took it. From him, I at least expected more. Like a text explaining or saying he wouldn't be here. Which was so un-Brady-like for him not to do that I began to get concerned again.

My phone vibrated on my nightstand, and I stared at it. I had forgotten to put it on silent. That was Brady. No one else had my number and would be texting me so late. Did I ignore it? Or read it? He was two hours late. But knowing Brady, there had to be an excuse.

I picked up the phone.

You awake?

Seriously? That's his text after not showing up like he said? I really should ignore it. I started to when I saw headlights pull into my drive then shut off. Did he really think I was coming outside at eleven?

I'm in bed. There. That would send him on his way.

I started to put the phone down when he replied.

I'm outside.

Rolling my eyes, I texted, I know. But I'm in bed.

I waited to see if he'd back out. He didn't. He continued to sit there. If this were any other guy, I'd think that he was assuming I would come running. But it was Brady, who knew better and was more respectful. Thoughtful.

Love isn't real. It sucks. I fucking hate it.

I read his words and a frown wrinkled my brow. What?

He wasn't making sense. Why was he talking about love? And had I ever heard him say *fucking* before?

You believe shit and you trust people. But they let you down and fuck everything up. They're selfish.

His newest text finally drew me out of bed. I put on a pair of flip-flops and headed down the hallway. My parents' bedroom door opened and my mom peeked out at me.

"What are you doing?" she asked. Her glasses were still perched on her nose, which meant she was awake reading.

"Brady is outside, and from his texts he seems really upset about something. I'm going to check on him. He doesn't sound like himself."

Mom nodded. "Okay. I'll listen out for Bryony."

"Thank you."

I didn't get the *be careful* or *be smart* lecture most girls got. The one I used to get back when I started dating. My parents knew that I was well aware of what could happen. I had lived through it.

I opened the door as my phone vibrated in my hand again. I didn't read this time. I just went to his truck.

When I opened the passenger-side door, the smell of beer surprised me. There were three empty bottles on the floorboard and one in the cup holder. What in the world was going on?

"What's wrong?" I asked him, closing the door behind me.

"Everything," he drawled. Four beers to most guys wasn't much, but for Brady, who never drank, it was a lot. I could hear the effect in his voice. He was slurring—for the first time in his life, I'd wager.

"You're drinking. And driving. It must be bad."

He let out a hard laugh and laid his head back on the seat. "Bad," he repeated, then laughed some more, but there was no real humor in it. There was bitterness there. And pain.

He reached for the beer and I took it away. "That's enough, I think. Why don't you tell me what happened."

He closed his eyes tightly as if he was blocking out something bad. Something he didn't want to remember. I sat there quietly, understanding that he needed time. This wasn't easy. Whatever it was had really done a number on him.

"I wanted to use my dad's truck tonight. So we could go around undetected. People wouldn't be looking for me that way. Give us some privacy in this small town." He stopped and laughed again. "Privacy. I don't give a fuck about privacy. They can all fucking know now! All of them! I'll put it on a damn billboard and they can fuck themselves. The whole damn lot. It's just football. Just motherfucking football. Means nothing. It's not what matters in life. What matters is having trust. A family that you trust." He slammed his palm on the steering wheel.

So this was about family? His family? What, did his dad

not let him use his truck? Surely that wasn't what all this was about.

"Brady, what happened?" I repeated my question.

He sighed and winced. "I went to his office. He was working on a Sunday. Who the hell works on a Sunday? Apparently my dad does. But he wasn't working." The look on Brady's face made me sick. My stomach knotted up. I hoped this wasn't going where I feared it would.

"Brady, no," I whispered, already seeing the pain so clear on his face to know this was going to end badly. Terribly.

"She was younger, blond, naked, and on his desk. His pants were down." He stopped and inhaled sharply. Just saying those words had to be like a knife being shoved in his chest. He had parents like mine. The ones everyone trusted and believed were perfect.

I didn't know what to say. If this had been me, was there anything that could have been said to ease my pain? No. The suffering would never end. It would ruin me. Moreso than Rhett had. Bryony had healed that, but could anything heal this?

"He didn't see me. They were too busy." He said the last word like a sour taste in his mouth. "And my mom was home cooking him his favorite dinner. The cake he loves so much was in the oven smelling up the house."

My heart was breaking. For Brady and his mother. These secrets never stayed a secret. They always found a way of coming out. This was a small town, and Brady was the golden boy. His family was the rock-solid type that everyone respected. It would all come tumbling down.

"And my biggest concern when I woke up this morning was a fucking football game. I've never had a real problem. Never faced something that changed my life." He turned his head and finally looked at me. "But you have. You lived through hell and came out okay. How did you survive?"

I wanted to hug him and tell him everything would be all right. But that was a lie you told children when they lost their pet. It wasn't the truth. No one had ever told me that. But my heart hurt for him, and fighting the urge to comfort him was hard. It wasn't what he needed, though. I knew that. My feelings for Brady had grown stronger with each day, and I never realized how seeing him in pain would affect me. Until now. I did what I had to do. I told him the truth. He'd been fed enough lies about life.

"You survive. You remember that life is hard. Shit happens and you have to get tough. The fairy tale from our childhood is gone. Living in it makes us weak. Your mom will need you, and you'll have to be strong for both of you."

"I don't know if I can."

I understood that feeling too. I'd had it often back then.

When I thought my life was over and I'd never make it through.

"You can. You just have to find it deep inside. It's there. The strength. We all have it, but it lies dormant until we need it. Then we have to look for it and use it."

CHAPTER 28

BRADY

My head was pounding when I opened my eyes. A pair of big blue eyes were staring back at me. Startled, I jumped, but she continued to stare. Her head tilted to the side. She looked a lot like her mother at that moment.

"Hey?" she whispered, still very close to my face.

I glanced down at my body and saw I was on a sofa in Riley's grandmother's house, covered in a yellow-and-blue afghan. Riley hadn't allowed me to drive last night, and I was glad. Not because I agreed that I was drunk but because I didn't want to go home. I didn't want to see my dad.

The sick knot returned, and I wanted to go back to sleep, where yesterday never happened.

"Have you seen Thomas?" an older lady asked me as she walked into the living room. She wasn't concerned that I was on her sofa.

"No," Bryony answered her, then she looked back at me. "Thomas wif Jesus," she said, still whispering.

I couldn't even begin to understand that, so I just nodded.

"Good morning, Brady. I hope you slept well," Mrs. Young said as she entered the room. I sat up on the sofa this time and wondered if she had known I was here. It had been late when we came inside last night.

"Uh, yes, ma'am. Thank you," I replied.

"No reason to hurry. I just woke Riley up. She'll be in here in a moment. I'm making some coffee. Do you want any?" It seemed as if Riley had told her I was here last night. She wasn't at all surprised.

"No, thanks. Not a coffee drinker," I replied.

"Good. Don't become one. It's the hardest habit to break. I drink way too much of it."

"Have you seen Thomas?"

Riley's mother turned to her own mother and patted her on the back. "Not this morning. Why don't we go get your breakfast started. He'll turn up sometime."

Bryony ran after them. "I some hungwy," she called out.

Riley's mother stopped and bent down to pick her up. "I'll bet you are," she replied.

Then they all left the room, and I got up and began to straighten where I had been sleeping.

"You going home?" Riley asked.

I turned to see her in the cut-off sweats she'd been wearing last night and a tank top. Her hair was messy from sleep, but she seemed unconcerned about that. I liked that about her.

"Yeah. I got to shower and change before school. I'm already going to miss morning workout. Don't care, but my father will."

That was a confrontation I was dreading. Looking at him was going to infuriate me. I couldn't just tell him what I knew. I had to decide how to tell my mom first. This was going to rock her world as much as he had mine. No, it would rock it more. Because he was her other half, the man she'd trusted for twenty years.

"Are you going to tell your mom?"

Eventually. "Not yet. I need to think this through. She is delicate."

Riley gave me a sad smile. "Just because she cooks your meals and takes care of the home doesn't make her weak. She's raised you, brought a girl into her home who faced a tragedy I can't begin to comprehend, and was a mother to her. She's tough. Give her that credit."

She was loving. But did that make her strong?

"I still need some time."

Riley nodded. "Okay. I'm here if you need me."

I wanted to hug her. Kissing wasn't real big on my list right now. My father had ruined that image for me. But having Riley in my arms sounded good.

With her mother, grandmother, and daughter in the next room, I decided against it. "Thanks for last night."

"Anytime."

I headed for the door and glanced back just before I walked out to see her watching me go. She even woke up beautiful. She wasn't trying to be fake. She was just her.

"I'll call you," I told her.

She just nodded.

Then I headed home.

My dad's truck was still in the drive when I pulled in. He was normally gone to work by now. My not being at home when he woke up had delayed that. He'd be inside right now waiting on me. Ready to question me and correct me. Bastard. He had no right to correct anyone.

He could go to hell for all I cared.

Slamming my truck door, all the anger from yesterday boiled to the surface and although I needed to calm down before I walked in that door to face him, I couldn't. I wanted to yell at him and let him see the hate in my eyes.

He opened the door before I got there, his face a mask of disappointment and fury. As if he had the right to feel either. I'd slept on a friend's sofa, and I'd be late to school. Neither of those things would destroy anyone. He couldn't say the same for what he'd done yesterday.

"Where have you been?" he barked at me.

"None of your fucking business," I replied as I tried to brush past him.

His hand grabbed my arm to stop me, and the strength in his grip wasn't pleasant. "Who the hell do you think you are? I make the rules in this house. You don't speak to me that way and you don't stay out all night."

I tried to jerk my arm free. Just being near him made me cringe. "Whatever," I said, snarling at him.

"You smell like beer," he replied with disbelief on his face. "Are you trying to throw away your future? You got this close and now you're going to toss it? For what? A girl who lies and sleeps around?"

He hadn't come looking for me because he had known where I was. Had Riley's mother called him? Probably. The asshole was throwing accusations at Riley, who had done nothing wrong. How dare he?

With a quick glance to make sure my mother wasn't standing anywhere near us, I leaned into him. "At least I'm not married and fucking a woman in my office," I spat and jerked my arm free this time from his grip. His face paled some, and I knew he understood what I was saying.

I stalked past him and toward the stairs just as Maggie was coming down them. She had a questioning look in her eyes, but she said nothing. She was someone else who would be affected by this. Her parents were both dead, thanks to her father, and this family was her only security. Dad had blown her world to shit too.

"We aren't done talking," Dad said from the bottom of the stairs.

"Want to fucking bet?" I shot back at him and slammed the door of the bathroom behind me.

He's a Handsome Thing,
Ain't He?

CHAPTER 29

RILEY

My doorbell rang an hour after Brady left. No one ever came to the door. I was hoping it wasn't Brady and he had made it to school without getting into a fistfight with his father.

Bryony ran to the door, her face all lit up with excitement. She wasn't used to company either, and this was going to be the highlight of her morning. Other than the fact that Brady had been sleeping on the sofa when she woke up.

I didn't actually know the pretty brunette at my door, but I knew of her. She was Brady's cousin. The girl who came to Lawton not talking and was now the reason West Ashby wasn't a complete dickhead.

"Hello," I said, knowing already why she was here.

Brady's return home hadn't gone well this morning. It was after eight and she should be at school.

"Hi, Riley?" she said, making sure she had the right person.

"Yes," I replied.

"I'm sorry for coming over like this, but I'm Maggie, Brady's cousin. And I know he slept here last night. That's not my business, but the scene I witnessed this morning has me concerned for him."

I stepped back and waved a hand for her to come inside. Bryony was by my side, peeking up at her from around my leg.

"Come on in," I told her.

She walked in and smiled down at Bryony.

"I wike your haywah," Bryony said shyly.

"Thank you. I like yours too. I always wanted blond curls. You have beautiful ones."

Bryony beamed at her. She loved her blond curls too. She often sat in front of the mirror just to brush them.

"My mother said she called the house and let Mrs. Higgens know Brady was here last night."

Maggie nodded. "Yes, but he's never done that before, and he smelled like beer. Which I'm fairly certain he's smelled like before." She paused and handed me what looked like a cake she was holding. "Aunt Coralee sent this. She said she'd been meaning to bring one over herself."

I took the cake from her. I couldn't tell her anything. This was Brady's to tell. Not mine. "Tell her thank you for me," I replied.

"I'm not here to ask you to tell me what's going on. I just need to know if he's okay," Maggie said.

I could answer that. "No, he's not."

Maggie frowned. "I was afraid of that. Things weren't good between him and Uncle Boone. But I've never seen them that way. I just don't know how to help."

She couldn't. No one could.

"Trust me when I tell you that you can't help him. He's got to do this alone. If he needs to open up, he will; otherwise just let him be."

She nodded. "Okay. I get that. Better than most, I guess. But I did need someone. West became my someone. I think everyone needs someone." She paused and looked directly at me. "I hope you're his."

I did too. "If I am, I won't let him down."

She smiled and looked back at the door. "I'm late for school. I guess I need to leave before my uncle is upset with me, too. Thanks for talking. It was nice to finally meet you," she said, then turned her attention to Bryony. "It was nice to meet you, too."

Bryony smiled brightly up at her. Then ducked behind my legs.

We said good-byes, and I closed the door behind Maggie. She was sweet, beautiful, and she obviously got the "not to be intrusive" thing. Brady was lucky to have her in his home with him. It would help when he was ready to open up.

"Can you go to Miller's and get me a pound of sugar? I think I'm gonna make some of my cherry cobbler for Lyla," Grandmamma said, smiling down at Bryony. Today Bryony was going to be my mother as a child again. We didn't have these days every day, but today Grandmamma had called her Lyla three times already. Bryony always seemed confused but had stopped arguing with her about her name.

"Sure," I told her. "Why don't we go see if your talk shows are on yet. I think it's time for *Dr. Phil*," I told her.

"I need to feed Thomas first," she argued.

"Let Bryo . . ." I paused and corrected myself. "Let Lyla do that. You know she loves to."

Grandmamma thought about it a minute, then nodded. "That's a good idea. She needs responsibility. Never hurt anyone."

I winked at Bryony when we had to play pretend with Grandmamma. She blinked hard with both eyes because she couldn't wink yet. Grinning, I turned on the television for Grandmamma and Bryony headed to the kitchen to pretend to feed a cat that didn't exist.

"I want Wywa appasauce," she said quietly when we got to the kitchen. On the days she was confused for Lyla, Grandmamma always gave her applesauce. It had been my mother's favorite snack as a baby. Bryony had figured this out.

"Okay," I replied, setting the cake down, then lifted her up into her high chair.

My mind was on Brady, though. He was facing school and friends with his soul shattered. Holding a secret like that had to feel like the weight of the world was on him. I couldn't be strong for him, though. No one could. He had to find that in himself. At least he wasn't alone.

"Do I like *Dr. Phil*?" Grandmamma called from the living room.

This was a bad day. Some days were better than others. Today she was confused about everything. I walked to the door and looked in on her. "Yes. He's brilliant and will have all kinds of good tips for you."

She nodded and covered her legs with the afghan we kept on the sofa. She had made it years ago. "He's a handsome thing, ain't he?" she commented. She said this every day when she watched him.

"Yes," I agreed, grinning, then stepped back to the

kitchen to pour Bryony some applesauce. I was sure I would be told to go get some more at Miller's for Lyla later today.

"Go pawk?" Bryony asked.

"Yes, we will go later today, after your nap," I assured her. It was getting colder every day, and I dreaded when we couldn't go to the park anymore. Bryony needed a swing here at home, so she could go to the backyard and enjoy herself for shorter amounts of time. The biting cold that was to come would keep us from walking to the park. She would hate that.

This Was the Only
Weapon I Had
CHAPTER 30

BRADY

Nash Lee was sitting in the desk next to mine when I walked into class. He wasn't grinning like normal. Which meant I was about to get drilled about not being at workout this morning. West was the only one who didn't mention it, and I had Maggie to thank for that. Everyone else was worried I was sick. That damn game was all they could think about.

"You good?" Nash asked as I sat down beside him. Same exact question I'd heard from Gunner, Asa, and Ryker. No, I was not fucking good. I'd never be fucking good again.

"Yeah," I lied, not saying anything else. I never missed

a practice or a workout. They all had at some point. So why couldn't I miss one without the damn inquisition?

"Coach was worried."

Coach had been waiting on me the moment I walked in the door this morning. I was aware he was worried. He, too, thought I was sick. He was ready to send me home to rest. A place where I didn't want to be. A place full of lies and deceit.

My father hadn't been there when I'd come out of the bathroom this morning. I'd almost expected him to be, but he had left for work. My mom had looked beyond worried, but I couldn't explain any of this to her. I wasn't sure how I ever would.

"You just never miss." Nash stated the obvious.

"I did today" was the only response he was getting. Jesus, couldn't they all back off? I didn't drill them when they missed. I respected their privacy.

Where was *my* respect, dammit?!

"Rifle said he saw your truck at Riley Young's. He was whispering it to Hunter, and I shut it down. That shit ain't true, but they're spreading crap and I wanted you to know. I can handle it if you want."

Rifle Hannon was a sophomore and didn't even know the real details about two years ago. He'd been in middle school, for crying out loud. He might be a good tight end, but he needed to keep his mouth fucking shut about me if he wanted playing time.

"I was there. But it's no one's fucking business," I said, looking straight ahead. Nash was my friend, but I was past caring what everyone thought of me. Of my choices. They sure acted as they pleased. Got drunk at the field party, fucked around with girls at school, took nothing seriously but football. I was tired of being the good one. I wasn't trying to make my dad proud anymore. I did not give one fuck.

"Gunner won't take that well," Nash said, as if I needed reminding.

I turned to him then and made sure he saw the look on my face. The one telling him just how many fucks I did not give. "I don't need Gunner's permission for shit."

Nash's eyes went wide and he nodded. I was surprising them all. And I didn't care. My team's feelings were no longer important to me. Friday night wasn't important to me. After the game wasn't important to me. My family was a joke. My mom, who deserved a man to love her and be good to her, was the only real thing in my life. That and my friendship with Riley. The others could kiss my ass.

When the class started, Nash thankfully fell silent and I tried to focus on what was being said and not ways to handle my father's sins. By the time it ended, I wasn't sure what the assignment was or anything we learned. My head wasn't there. It was at my dad's office, where he'd ruined my life.

I attempted to make it through the next class, and when it was a replica of the first one I gave up and walked out the front door to my truck. I headed for the park. At some point Riley and Bryony would be there, and I'd be waiting. It was the only place I could go.

Gunner would hear about Riley before the day was over. I didn't care. He could get angry all he wanted. Fact was, his brother was a douche bag and needed to be called out for what he'd done. I wasn't protecting that asshole anymore. If Gunner wanted to, then fine. His brother had fucked him over too. And I understood that shit about family coming first, but if I could hate my father for his sins, then Gunner could hate his brother and recognize the fact that he'd lied.

My phone lit up and I glanced down to see West's name on the screen. Picking it up, I read, You need me?

I'd say he wouldn't understand. I could throw the phone down and say *fuck it* and ignore him. But he'd lost his dad recently and that hadn't been easy. He understood pain. He'd lived through it before me. I got why he kept it to himself now. Not having to talk about it was easier.

No. But thanks, I replied, then drove out of the parking lot. I wasn't hungry and doubted I would be again.

Here if you need me was his response.

I appreciated that. But I wouldn't need him. I needed my dad to be the man he pretended to be. I needed my dad not to have fucked that blond woman. That's what I fucking needed.

The park was only four miles from the school. I parked and waited in my truck. It was only noon, and I knew it was after lunch and Bryony's nap that they came here. But I had nowhere else to go. I laid my head back and closed my eyes. Silence was good. Here I had no questions and I wasn't expected to perform.

Friday night I wasn't sure I could play. My heart wasn't in it and I no longer cared. The idea of how angry my dad would be made me want to skip it. Just leave town and hide. Make him feel some pain. Some disappointment. It was nothing compared to what I was dealing with.

Problem with that was I would let others down. West, who never missed a game, even while his dad was dying. My mom, who was my biggest fan. My coach, who had worked with me since junior high and believed in me. This town. Although it wasn't perfect, they weren't all to blame. That was all on my father.

I'd play the game. But winning it was another matter

altogether. I didn't think I had it in me. My drive for success was gone. I feared it always would be. My dad had made my life about him. I wanted to let him down. I wanted to destroy him like he'd destroyed me. This was the only weapon I had.

But could I hurt others to use it?

CHAPTER 31

RILEY

Brady's truck was the first thing I noticed when Bryony and I strolled up to the park entrance. He was supposed to be in school. This wasn't a good sign. Bryony pointed at his truck, remembering it, then waved as if he could see her.

I wasn't sure if I should walk over to him or just go into the park. We were a secret, I thought. But at this point maybe we weren't anymore. Or maybe he didn't care. If he didn't care, that meant he was giving up on the game. The championship. I got where his head was. I understood it, but he'd regret that later. I had regrets and I wished I didn't. I wished someone had helped me see things differently.

I went ahead and took Bryony into the park. Brady

could come talk to me if that was his choice. We needed to talk. Especially if he was giving up on his dream. But talking here wasn't the best idea. Putting Bryony in his truck and riding around wasn't happening either.

I bent down and let Bryony out of the stroller, and she squealed with delight and headed for the small slide she loved so much. I took my normal seat on the bench closest to the slide and watched her, although my thoughts were with that truck parked outside the gate.

Footsteps let me know he was headed my way, so I turned to see him. He looked lost. Defeated. Confused. And I wanted to just hug him. A guy like Brady with the life of dreams he had lived so far wasn't emotionally prepared for this turn of events. It was unfair, but then so was life. Finding that out sooner rather than later would help him. It may not feel like it at the moment, but one day he'd understand.

"School too much?" I asked as he stopped beside me then sat down.

"Yeah" was his response.

I didn't say more. He had come here looking for me. That was obvious. If he wanted to sit in silence, we could do that, too. Whatever worked. He knew what he needed.

"I can't focus enough to play Friday night."

I had been afraid of this.

"But all I can think is, West played when his dad was dying of cancer. He played when his heart was breaking. How can I not do the same? For him if no one else?"

"I think you just answered yourself. West is your best friend. You respect him. He didn't let the team down when his world was falling apart." I didn't add *and neither will you* because he had to make that decision.

We sat in silence for a few minutes. He was thinking. I let him.

When he finally spoke, he leaned forward resting his elbows on his knees. "I want to hurt my dad. This would hurt him."

As much as I understood that, I also understood regret. Something Brady didn't know about yet, but he would eventually. "Is hurting your dad more important than not letting West down? The team? Yourself?"

He ran his hands over his face and groaned. "No. They don't deserve that."

I agreed with him completely.

"Then you know what you have to do. There isn't really a question. It's how will you focus on the game and do it? You need to figure that out."

He turned his head and looked at me. "Will you come? I'm going to need you after the game."

I hadn't been to a game in two years. I wasn't sure this

was a good idea. "The others, the town, they won't like it."

"I don't care what they like. If you're there, I can win. I can remember what is important. But I need you there."

Facing this town and all the people in it wasn't terrifying anymore. I wasn't the same young girl they had run off. I was strong and I knew the truth. To me that was all that mattered. They could believe what they wanted.

"Will my being there hurt the game because of the others?"

He shook his head. "I'll have West, and if we need to, the two of us can win that game."

Then I'd go. "I'll be there."

He let out a sigh, and a smile that didn't really meet his eyes curled on his lips. "Thanks. That's going to help."

I wanted to know how he'd handled his dad this morning, but if he wasn't going to talk about it I wasn't going to ask. He needed his space and I was there to give it to him. I would only enter the space he needed me to.

"I cursed at my dad today. More than once."

No wonder Maggie had come over. I thought about telling him, but I didn't. She could tell him if she wanted him to know. I wasn't getting involved in the family dynamics.

"I'd say you could sit with Maggie, but she'll sit with my parents. I don't want to see my dad when I look at you."

"I'll sit far away from them," I told him.

He nodded. "Thank you. For last night. For this. I know it's asking a lot."

I shrugged. "It isn't. I'm not the same girl who left this town. I found my strength. They can't hurt me now."

His hand closed over mine. The touch made my entire arm tingle, and I let the warmth soothe me. Turning my attention back to Bryony, I watched as she played with a little boy whose nanny brought him every Monday and Wednesday afternoon at this time. She had spoken to me a few times, assuming I, too, was a nanny since I was so young. I didn't correct her; I just let her talk. No reason to make her act weird around me and possibly not come around with the boy when Bryony was here. Small towns could be judgmental, and it fell on the innocent too many times.

"Looks like she has a friend," Brady said.

"His name is Luke, and he's three. She plays with him twice a week here. I wish she could go to preschool next year. She loves being around other kids. But if we are still in this town, that isn't possible."

His hand squeezed mine "We will make sure she gets that."

We. As in him and me? When did we become a *we*?

I didn't ask or bring it up, but I pondered it. The rest of the time we sat there in silence, speaking only about Bryony and other things that had nothing to do with football or his father. Eventually he laced his fingers through mine and we just enjoyed each other, I cool fall air, and the laughter of the kids. In that moment I wasn't a single teenage mom and he wasn't a guy whose dad was about to ruin his family. We were just us and life was okay. For the moment.

CHAPTER 32

BRADY

I made it to practice that afternoon and avoided the questions. The truth was, I was there because of Riley. She had made me see that I had to do this and that I could. If she was willing to brave this town and come to a game alone, then I could show up and play ball. Problem was, I wanted everyone else to fuck off and get out of my face.

Coach watched me closely at the first, expecting me to play like shit, I guess. But after I channeled my anger into the practice, I was more aggressive and played better. I was getting slapped on the back and shit when it was over; no one seemed to care that I'd played harder and faster. Or even why. Because they didn't care. It was all about winning.

West met me at my truck when I walked out of the field house. He might have been the only one on the field today to see the difference for what it really was. "Good practice. You want to go get some dinner?" In other words, not go home and blow off our families.

"Yeah," I replied. "I'll let my mom know."

He nodded. "My mom's at her mother's again in Louisiana." She had been doing that since his father's death. I knew it concerned him, but like with everything he didn't talk about it much. I knew he had Maggie, and he talked to her, so I didn't worry.

"Where did you go today?" he asked, climbing into the passenger side of my truck. He was leaving his car here, apparently.

"To the park to see Riley," I replied honestly. I wasn't hiding her. I had to hide my dad's fucked-up secret, but I wasn't hiding Riley like that.

"You like her a lot, then."

I nodded. "Yeah, I do."

"When it happens, it happens. Can't help that."

And I didn't want to help it. I wanted to change the past and give her a life here. Let everyone see the truth and support her. I wanted Bryony to get to go to fucking preschool and play with the other kids. That was what I wanted.

"Rhett took a lot away from her," West said. He knew if

I believed her, then she was telling the truth. He trusted me.

"He's a cocksucker."

West chuckled. "I guess he is. We were young then and caught up in his local fame. Believing him was easy."

"Believing him was wrong," I corrected.

He nodded. "Yeah, it was. The little girl seem okay?"

"Bryony. Her name is Bryony, and she's a great kid. Happy and well adjusted. Riley is a wonderful mom."

We didn't say much more before we got to the Den for dinner. It was the one place we'd always have a table and get 20 percent off our meal because we were on the team. Plus their burgers were the best in town.

"You and your dad okay?" he asked right before we got out of the truck. Maggie had to have told him about the fight this morning. I could get pissed at her, but then I thought about how I told Riley all my shit. I understood Maggie's need to talk to someone and why it was West.

"No. We're not" was the only answer he was getting. Then I stepped out of the truck and headed for the door. Not waiting on him or answering any more questions.

"Don't be mad at Maggie," he said, catching up to me.

"I'm not. I get it."

He didn't respond as we went inside and got a table immediately. Serena was there with Kimmie, and I wanted to leave at the sight of them, but I decided I'd ignore them and get my food.

"Hey, boys," Serena called, waving over to us.

We both ignored her, and I shot West a look. He had messed around with Serena enough and hurt Maggie with it. He wasn't about to look her way.

"Ever wonder where you'd be without Maggie?" I asked him.

He glanced up from the menu, which we already knew by heart. "Lost. Fucking lost."

Yeah. I got that. "Funny how that happens. One day you're good on your own. Then, bam, you need someone. They walk into your world and you need them."

West studied me a moment, then shook his head. "You're sunk. Welcome to the club."

I could argue with him and say my situation was different. That Riley and I were just good friends. Who kissed and held hands and possibly more. But I would be lying. Leaving for college didn't sound so good anymore. Facing that without her scared me. Especially right now. I wasn't ready to think that way.

If I told Riley that, she would freak out. She was insistent that I follow my dream and that my dream was football. She'd be right. It had been since I was a kid. But I needed to remember if it was my dream originally or one that my dad pushed onto me. What if I had other dreams? What if football wasn't what I was meant to do?

"Swear to God, if she comes over here I'm walking out," West said under his breath.

"I'll handle it," I told him.

He smirked. "Yeah, Mr. I'm Too Nice to Break Up with a Girl I Don't Like Because It Will Hurt Her Feelings will handle it."

He had a point. But I wasn't that Brady anymore. That Brady died yesterday. Along with his innocence. And possibly his dream.

"I'll handle it," I repeated.

West shrugged, looking amused. I almost hoped she would walk over here so I could prove it.

In the end, what good would that really do? Make me feel fucking better, that's what.

You Look a Lot Like
Your Mommy

CHAPTER 33

RILEY

Went out to dinner with West after practice. Didn't want to go home was the text I got from Brady around eight that night.

How was practice? I wanted to know. He'd been ready to just quit earlier today, and I couldn't let him do that.

Good. I played out my anger and it made me a better quarterback. Aggressive.

Smiling, I thought about Brady as aggressive and the two didn't mix. Glad you found a way to make it work.

He had a lot to face over the next few weeks. I understood why football wasn't at the top of that list. His mother was. The pain she'd suffer. It was killing him to think about her hurting. Her future wasn't going to be easy. Brady knew that.

I looked over at Bryony sleeping beside me. So peaceful and secure. She didn't have that concern yet; one day she would ask about her father. Where was he? Who was he? And I would need something to tell her. The actual truth was too much for a child. I never wanted her to feel like a mistake.

I wish I had seeing you at school every day to look forward to. That text was sweet but just reminded me how I'd never fit into his world. We could kiss and hold hands, but I wasn't a teenage girl with a crush on a boy anymore. That would never be my first concern.

I stared at his words, trying to think of a response that didn't sound harsh or uncaring. He was hurting right now and my lecture on why I couldn't be that girl for him didn't seem appropriate at the moment.

Finally I texted, You're stronger than you know. And if you want to see me after practice you know where I am.

That was enough for now. I was the only person who knew his secret. He needed me and I could be there for him. But he would heal from this. He would move on and he would go live his life. I needed never to forget that.

Can you go to dinner tomorrow night? We could take Bryony too.

Where? To the Den, where everyone in town would see us? Gunner flipping out was not what he needed right now.

That might get sticky. With only three days to go before the game.

This town wouldn't just accept me because Brady did. They didn't forget and they didn't forgive. I knew that more than anyone. Although I had nothing to be forgiven for. Unless telling the truth was offensive.

I don't want to hide you. Gunner can get over it.

My heart did a little squeeze and flutter from his words. That didn't change the facts, but it made me feel good. You don't need that battle right now.

Bryony rolled over and curled up against my body. I smelled her hair, then kissed her head.

I need you was his response.

How was I supposed to argue with that?

Okay, I replied. Because if he was ready for this, then so was I.

The next day after our park visit I strolled Bryony over to the pharmacy to get Grandmamma's prescriptions. The door opened before we got to it and a familiar face walked out. It was Willa Ames. I remembered her from my childhood, and just a month or so ago I'd given her a ride. She'd been walking home from a field party.

"Hello," she said to me with a genuine smile on her face. Either she was still grateful for the ride or Gunner hadn't yet filled her head with bad things about me.

"Hey," I replied, and Bryony caught her attention. She bent down to eye level with Bryony.

"You look a lot like your mommy," she told her, and Bryony smiled brightly. "What's your name?"

"Bwony," she told her with pride.

"That's a beautiful name. I'm Willa, and it's very nice to meet you."

I watched Willa talk to my daughter, and it was obvious she knew Bryony was my child, not my sister. The kindness in her eyes made me like her even more. If she was still hooking up with Gunner, I'd be surprised. She seemed too smart for that.

"Are you homeschooling still? Haven't seen you at school. I hoped maybe you would eventually show up."

What all did Willa Ames know about me?

"I have my grandmother to take care of while my parents work, and Bryony. School isn't an option for me. Besides, no one wants me there."

Willa raised an eyebrow. "I do. Very few females there I'd be willing to call a friend."

Did she mean she would be my friend? How had this girl not heard all about me by now? Was she a recluse?

"I wouldn't be an option either. You must not have heard my story."

A small frown tugged at her lips. "I've heard it. I just believe there's some truth and facts missing."

I liked this girl. Now I really hoped she wasn't messing around with Gunner Lawton. He'd ruin her. Even if he and Willa had been friends as kids. He was different now.

"Thanks. You may be the only one in town who thinks that," I replied.

Her frown turned into a small, knowing smile. "Oh, I don't know. I think maybe Brady Higgens may believe as I do."

What? Had Brady told her something?

"I've got to get this medicine to my nonna. She's dealing with a migraine. But don't be a stranger. Maybe come to a game. I could always use a friend to sit with."

All I could do was nod. This was surprising and confusing. Were she and Brady friends? And if they were, why hadn't he told me?

"Bye-bye," Bryony called out, and Willa turned and waved at Bryony. "Bye!"

I opened the door and pushed Bryony inside. When I had given Willa a ride, she hadn't been that nice and open. She had been closed off and sad. It was as if this town had helped her. The town that had torn me apart seemed to have made her a happier person.

"Canny!" Bryony announced, pointing to the candy aisle. I would have to get her something to keep her from pitching a royal fit. I walked over and picked up some yogurt-covered raisins. They were the least of all the evils, I figured.

"Be good while I get the medicine; then you can have the candy," I told her.

She made a move like she was zipping up her lips, and I laughed. In moments like these I couldn't imagine my life any other way.

My Life Isn't Gunner's to Control

CHAPTER 34

BRADY

Another successful practice. Anger really made me better. I wasn't worried about anyone or the rest of the team. I just zeroed in on me and everyone seemed to like it. Tomorrow was Wednesday, and my dad normally came to Wednesday practices. If he did this week, I was walking out. I didn't want this to be about him.

If I began to feel like this was about him, I'd quit just to hurt him. It would never hurt him as much as he was hurting us, but it was all I had as ammunition. I focused on seeing Riley tonight, and that made it easier to push thoughts of my father out of my head.

"Excellent practice," Coach said as he walked past me.

"Whatever has gotten into you, keep it. Best you've played in your life, and I didn't know it could get much better."

The bitterness of what had gotten into me simmered, and I could only nod before heading to the field house to shower and change. I wasn't about to go home and face my father. I was avoiding him the best I could. He hadn't been home last night when I got there, so I went to bed after hugging my mom and assuring her I was okay.

It had taken all my willpower not to slam my bedroom door and lock it when I went to my room. He wasn't home, and it was after eight. His working late and after hours wasn't actually working. It was fucking. Damn son of a bitch.

I tossed my clothes into my bag and quickly showered then dressed in my jeans and a clean T-shirt. I needed to see Riley. She'd calm me down. I wanted to hit something or someone. Anything to get all this aggression out of me.

"You okay?" Gunner asked, walking beside me as I left the field house.

"Yeah," I replied, not wanting to get into anything with him.

"You're different. Angry. Shit's going on and you're keeping it to yourself. Reminds me of . . . me."

Nothing about me was like him. He was a cold, heartless bastard when he wanted to be. I was never like that.

"I'm good. Just got things on my mind. Don't want to talk about it."

He sighed. "Been there. But I found someone to talk to, and she was what kept me from drowning or losing my goddamn mind. You need to talk."

I was talking. With the one girl he hated above all others. Telling him that would shut him the fuck up.

"I've got someone to talk to. Don't need anyone's approval."

"You're acting like this is my fault. What the hell did I do?"

He'd let his family ruin Riley's life. He was still doing it. That was what he fucking did. I inhaled deeply and tried to calm down. Confronting him about this right here while I was raw from my dad's bullshit wasn't the way to handle it.

"Just back off and give me space," I told him as we reached my truck.

"Y'all good?" West asked, stepping out of his truck to look at both of us.

"No, he's fucked-up about something. Can't you see it?" Gunner replied.

"I think backing off and letting him be is the best idea right now," West told him.

I jerked open my door and climbed in. I'd thank West later. Tonight I wanted away from Lawton. All of it.

* * *

Pulling up outside Riley's house, I wondered if Gunner had followed me. I almost hoped he had. I was tired of secrets. There were too many in my life right now.

Riley shouldn't have to be a secret, and the Lawtons owed her an apology and a chance to live free again in this town. The front door opened just as I climbed out of the truck, and Riley stepped out wearing a pair of tight jeans that showed off her amazing legs with a blue sweater that matched her eyes. Bryony wasn't with her, though.

"Hey," I said as I walked to meet her.

"You didn't have to come to the door."

"Yeah, I did. You deserve that."

She blushed and her eyes lit up. "Bryony ate with my parents and she didn't get her nap in today. Mom said to leave her here so she could go to bed early."

So it was just us. As much as I'd been looking forward to spending time with Bryony tonight, it might be best that she wasn't with us. My anger was still there under the surface, and if anyone confronted me about this, it was going to get ugly.

"Next time we'll go earlier for her sake," I promised.

I opened the truck door for Riley, and she climbed inside. Just as I closed it, Gunner's truck rode past the house. He slowed and our gazes locked. This was it. He knew now, and I would deal with it. At least there would be one less secret in my life.

I turned and headed for my door. When I climbed inside I thought about not telling her what had just happened. But it was going to come out and there would be a confrontation tonight. Gunner was too hotheaded for there not to be.

"Gunner just drove by," I told her, then started the truck.

"Do I need to get out?"

I turned to look at her. "No. My life isn't Gunner's to control."

Her worried frown made me want to lean over and kiss it away.

"You have too much on you right now to deal with this, too."

This was the least of my worries. My mother's world being torn apart and destroyed made Gunner's temper tantrum seem mute.

"He needs to get over it," I told her. "Now is as good a time as any for him to deal and grow up."

She let out a small laugh. "It won't be that easy," she told me.

"I don't care about easy. I care about you."

The way she seemed to ease and lean closer to me meant my being completely honest was the way to go. She liked that. I did too.

My phone lit up, and I glanced down at it to see Gunner's name. I clicked ignore and headed for Rossi's. It was an Italian place in town that cost more and the high school crowd didn't visit often. I wasn't in the mood to throw us out there in front of Serena and her bunch.

"You like Italian?" I asked her.

She nodded. "Yes, but Rossi's costs too much."

"It's worth it."

CHAPTER 35

RILEY

I had only eaten at Rossi's with my parents on Sunday afternoons and twice when I was dating Gunner. It was one of the more expensive places to eat around here. I had a feeling that was why Brady had chosen it. To give us some privacy.

I saw his phone light up again, and he glanced at it and ignored it. Then he stuck it in his pocket and continued to look at the menu.

"Is it still Gunner?" I asked him, worried about how this was affecting him.

"No, that was West. Probably warning me about Gunner."

"If you need to answer their calls, I'm fine with you stepping outside."

He shook his head. "All I need to do is help them win a football game. Otherwise they can suck it."

That was a very un-Brady-like thing for him to say. He was becoming less and less Brady-like. His father's infidelity was slowly eating at him. I wanted him to win the championship, but I also wanted him to be okay mentally. This was too much for him to cover up.

I studied the menu and decided on the lasagna before closing it and taking a drink of my Coke. I didn't want to harp on this, but he needed to get it off his chest. Holding all this in wasn't good for him.

When he closed his menu and met my gaze, he winked, as if he didn't have a care in the world and this were a normal date. Not one that could possibly blow up at any minute if Gunner Lawton followed us here and walked in that door.

"How was the park today? Bryony make any new friends?"

He wanted to talk about easy stuff. For now I would let him.

"There was a little girl around her age there with her grandmother. They played some before we had to leave. As it gets colder it's going to be harder to go to the park. I wish we had a swing in the backyard, where I could at least take her out when it is the sunniest and let her play some. She'll miss having other friends, but I can play with her. I thought about building her a fort or something like that."

Brady nodded. "She'd like a place out back to play. That's a good idea. Hopefully you can put her in preschool next year. It'd be great for her to play with the other kids."

He actually cared about this, and that made me want to tear up and cry. Bryony hadn't had anyone other than me and my parents in her life. Having someone else that cared meant more than he would ever know. Even if it was temporary.

"The game is home Friday right?" I asked him.

He nodded. "Yeah. You still good with going?"

I took a drink, then decided to tell him about Willa Ames.

"A month or so ago I picked a girl up on the side of the road walking home from a field party," I began.

"Willa," he added. He already knew.

"How did you know?" I asked him.

"Gunner told me about that night."

Figures. "Well, anyway, I saw her today at the pharmacy. She spoke to Bryony and she seemed to know that she was my daughter. Most people assume she's my sister. She was kind and basically asked me to come to a game and sit with her sometime. I know when I gave her a ride she was messing around with Gunner, so I wasn't sure what to think of all that."

He leaned back in his seat and smiled. "Sounds like Willa. And as a matter of fact she and Gunner are an item. She's changed him a good bit now, but even as kids those two fit. They were a matching set. Still are, it seems. She just started back to school two weeks ago. She had a short homeschooling time after some shit went down with the Lawtons. Ms. Ames was trying to protect her. But she's back now."

"That nice girl is dating Gunner?" I asked, a little surprised.

He nodded. "Yep. They had a rough patch and some issues to work through. Gunner's family is blown to hell. Not sure what all you know about that, but he's had a bad time of it. She's been there for him through it all."

Gunner dating Willa seemed like an odd fit to me. Gunner was selfish and self-absorbed. Willa had been so kind and gentle. Nothing about them matched up.

"What happened with his family?" I asked, not sure I wanted to know all this.

Brady started to tell me when the waiter appeared and we ordered our food. He left some bread on the table just as Brady's gaze fell on something over my shoulder and anger burned so bright I turned to see who he was looking at. I expected to see Gunner, but it wasn't.

It was a blond woman on the arm of a handsome man in a suit. The woman was wearing a clingy black dress that hit midthigh and silver heels that drew attention to her legs. The man whispered in her ear, and she laughed.

"That's her." Brady's voice sounded like hard, cold ice. I shivered.

"Who?" I asked turning back to him. His eyes blazed and his fists were clenched on the table as if he were ready to swing a punch at any time.

"The woman who was fucking my dad."

Oh. Oh no.

I turned back to look at her and saw there was a diamond on her left hand and the man sitting across from her also wore a wedding ring. It seemed that not only was one family going to be destroyed, but two were.

"I can't stay here," he said, his tone still so void of anything resembling Brady that I could barely recognize it.

"Of course," I replied, getting my purse and standing up.

"I'll tell the waiter. Meet me at the door," he said, and I obeyed, looking to see the woman one more time on my way out.

She was smiling at the man across from her as if she were in love. No one would guess otherwise. Was life really this jaded and sick? Did people fall in love and get married, then so easily throw it away for sex? Was one sex partner just not enough?

The woman turned to look my way, but her gaze traveled right past me, and I saw then: the emptiness in her eyes. The place where you should see one's soul. She had none. That made sense. She was out for herself. Nothing more. The man across from her had no idea, and I felt a twinge of sadness for this person I'd never meet.

Right when I got to the door, Brady was behind me. He had moved quickly. Like we were running from hell. His hand rested on my lower back as he opened the door for me to exit.

"I'm sorry about this," he said, his voice warming a touch.

"Don't be. I understand."

"Pizza okay with you?" he asked.

I was hungry, but I doubted he was.

"Can we get one to go and then sit somewhere alone and eat it? I think right now that's what you need."

He nodded. "Yeah. It is."

*That's the Best Pizza
I've Ever Had*

CHAPTER 36

BRADY

I hadn't wanted to talk much in the truck, and Riley seemed to get that. She didn't push me or ask questions. After going inside to grab the pizza, I drove us to the field. No one would be there on a Tuesday night. It was away from everything, and it was somewhere we could go undetected.

"Haven't been to this field in a long time," she said when I parked out in the clearing.

That wasn't exactly the truth. "Remember, I saw you back in August. You came here."

She ducked her head and stared at her hands. "Yes, but after seeing your welcoming face I left quickly. Never made it to the actual party. Which was a good thing. I'm not sure what I had been thinking."

I reached over and covered her hand with mine. "I'm sorry about that. I was a dick."

She shrugged. "You were reacting the way any of the guys would. You are Gunner's friend. I had no business trying to come here."

I hated that she felt that way.

"I was a dick," I repeated.

A laugh escaped her, and she nodded. "Yes, you were."

"Glad we can agree on that," I said. Then reached in the back to grab a blanket I kept there in case of emergencies. Or other things.

"Here, take this. It's cold tonight. I'll get the pizza and Coke."

"You have a blanket in the truck?" she asked, sounding amused.

I smirked. "Don't read too much into it."

Then she really laughed. "Okay. I'll keep that in mind."

We headed to the moonlit grass, and she chose a log by one of the bonfire sites. We wouldn't be lighting it tonight. But it was where the best seating was.

She wrapped the blanket around her and sat down. "I'll share if you need it," she said.

I might take her up on that after pizza. The idea of

getting under a blanket with her out here alone was nice. More than nice. Helped erase my fucked-up family issues from my head.

I opened up a Coke and handed it to her, then sat the box down and put a piece of pizza on a paper plate they'd given me with the order. "Here you go."

She took it. "This is nicer anyway. No waiters to interrupt us. The smell of fall and greasy pizza to go with it. My kind of dinner."

Being alone with her was my kind of dinner. "Glad you think so. Hell of a lot cheaper," I said, getting the laugh out of her I was trying for.

We ate in silence for a few minutes, and I liked watching her chew. It was cute. When she finished her first slice, I started to put mine down and get her more, but she beat me to it.

"So, if Willa and Gunner are a thing, she knows about me. Why was she so nice?"

"Because she's Willa. She also has a very low opinion of Rhett, and she's smarter than the rest of us. She met you and picked up right away that you weren't what we all assumed."

Riley smiled and took a bite.

"You ready to hear about the Lawton drama?" I asked her, needing to get my mind off that woman at the restaurant.

She nodded.

"Rhett came back asking for his inheritance or part of it a little over a month ago. His dad was going to give it to him because Rhett was the heir to the Lawton fortune. But come to find out Gunner's mother spoke up and Rhett isn't the heir. Neither is their father. Gunner is. Gunner's father isn't Rhett's father. It's . . . his grandfather. When his grandfather passed, he left it all to Gunner, although he was young then. His father was just to maintain it until Gunner was of age. His mother blew all that out of the water, though. Now Gunner controls it all."

The pizza was forgotten in her lap. "What?" she asked, sounding as amazed as I had. "You mean Gunner's grandfather is his father, so his mother—"

"His mother slept with her father-in-law. Yes."

"Wow."

I nodded. "Yeah. Rhett was raised to think it was all his and took off when he heard the truth. Gunner has had a hard time dealing with all of it. His dad packed his bags and filed for divorce. Gunner's mom is in France now, staying with a friend because she needs distance. So Gunner lives at home alone except for Ms. Ames being there to feed him and take care of the house."

Riley shook her head in disbelief. "I had heard a little. Mostly that he had inherited everything and his dad had left town. Not much else. Why doesn't the whole town know all this?"

I shrugged because I was surprised by that as well. "Gunner has kept it quiet. His parents aren't talking, and neither is Rhett."

"Jesus, that's got to be hard on him," she said, sounding truly worried about Gunner. A guy who had helped make her life a living hell. She didn't hold grudges and had the ability to hurt for others. Even the ones who had hurt her. If I weren't already completely taken with her, that one simple fact would have been all it took to send me over the edge.

"It's not been easy, but he's had Willa. She's helped him survive."

"I like her even more now."

That was what had drawn me to Riley. I realized it in this moment. Her heart. She had a really big heart. She was honest and kind. She wasn't bitter and vindictive when many people would be. The day I'd given her a ride in the storm and I'd seen her with Bryony, her only worry had been for her daughter. You can't hide goodness. Hers was there, shining bright. It got to me. She got to me.

"You would be good friends if given the chance."

"Maybe I'll sit with her at the game. If she's not worried about Gunner, then I don't guess we should be."

The idea of Riley sitting with Willa made me laugh.

Gunner's reaction to that would be priceless, but I also knew him well enough to know that he wouldn't upset Willa. He loved her more than he loved Rhett.

"You think that's funny?" she asked.

"No, I think it's awesome," I assured her.

She took another bite of pizza, then set her plate down. "That's the best pizza I've ever had."

She meant more than that. I could see it in her eyes. It was being here with me that made it the best pizza. I agreed with her completely.

The Lawton Bunch Isn't
So Tight Anymore

CHAPTER 37

RILEY

I was anxious most of the day. I kept my phone close to me all morning and waited on a call from Brady. I knew he would face Gunner today, and I was worried about him. He didn't need that right now.

It had rained all day, so when Bryony woke up from her nap there would be no playtime. I gave her crayons and a coloring book and let her color beside me while I worked on my schoolwork. I used my extra time to get ahead, and when Mother came into the room to remind me of Bryony's afternoon snack I realized how much time had passed. School was over and still no call or text from Brady.

When I'd gotten Bryony to her high chair and given her

some applesauce, I turned to ask Mom to watch her for me for just an hour. I was going to take the car and go to meet Brady after practice. I needed to know he was okay.

Maybe it was because she was a mother or because I was easy to read, but the moment she turned around she said, "Go on. I've got her. You've been working all day and need a break. Tell Brady I said hello."

I walked over to her and hugged her tightly. "Thank you."

She held me against her. "Of course. It's what mothers are for. I love you, and I like seeing you live a little. Does my heart good."

"I love you too," I told her.

"Wuv you too!" Bryony called from her high chair, and we both smiled and turned to see her grinning at us with applesauce all over her face.

"Mom will be thrilled she's eating applesauce if she comes in here and sees this."

I laughed and agreed.

"She's going to ask you to get some chocolate from Miller's to take to Mrs. Bertha for tea tomorrow. Just nod your head and go on. She's been on that line of thinking for an hour now."

"Who's Mrs. Bertha?" I asked, thinking that sounded new.

"A neighbor we had when I was in elementary school.

She moved away by the time I was twelve. Mom used to have tea with her every Sunday."

"Tomorrow is Thursday."

Mom let out a soft laugh. "Don't tell her that, either."

Life with Grandmamma sure was interesting.

I headed for the living room, and sure enough, there she sat with her afghan over her legs watching television. "If you're going out, get me some of that dark chocolate from Miller's. Told your momma, but she still ain't gone. They're gonna close soon. I can't go to Bertha's empty-handed tomorrow."

"Yes, ma'am," I replied and headed out the door.

"Don't forget to let Thomas back inside," she called out behind me.

Not sure how I was going to manage letting a cat that had been dead so long it was dust now back in the house, but I replied with another "Yes, ma'am."

I rarely drove the Mustang. Bryony liked for us to walk and wasn't a big fan of the car seat. So it was nice to get behind the wheel and drive in silence. I loved my family and my life. I was thankful for it. But a day dealing with a grandmother with Alzheimer's, a toddler, and schoolwork was mentally draining. This was normally my way of getting away for an hour and regrouping and relaxing. However, today I was tense and nervous.

It wasn't like Brady had promised to call me or text me today. He had kissed me before we'd gone back to the truck last night, and we had taken our time with it. Then it had been the short drive home and a good night. No promises or plans.

Still, I was worried about him.

It was time for practice to be over, and I didn't want Gunner to spot me in the parking lot, so I found a spot far enough away that I wouldn't be obvious but I could still seem them.

Gunner's truck was the closest to the field house, so he'd get to his truck first and be gone. Which worked out well for me. I watched the guys all leaving and only saw West as he climbed in his truck and left. Still no Brady or Gunner, and I began to get nervous. Surely West wouldn't have left if he thought there had been a problem.

A knock on my window startled me, and I turned around in my seat to see West, who I had just watched drive off, parked beside me and standing at my window.

Crap. I was terrible at incognito.

Rolling down my window I dreaded this. I should have stayed home and waited. My worry got the best of me.

"They're talking. Could be a while," West said.

"He saw us last night," I told him.

"I know. But things are different for Gunner now. The Lawton bunch isn't so tight anymore."

I nodded, understanding what he meant.

"You being here might not be the best idea, though. Brady will come to you when he's ready."

"Are they going to be okay?"

West chuckled. "If they tie up, Brady will take him. Gunner knows that. It's fine."

I still didn't want them tying up.

"Go home. Trust me. It's better for Brady."

West didn't hate me. He wasn't threatening me and there were no evil glares. Maybe things were different now.

"Okay," I agreed.

He gave me a nod, then went back to his truck but didn't start it up. He was waiting on me to leave like he had suggested. I did as he said and drove out. I didn't head to the house, though. I still needed a break from the day. So I just drove and waited for Brady to call or text.

It was after six, just before I was back at the house, when my phone rang.

"Hello," I said.

"Hey. West said you came by looking for me. Sorry it took me so long to get out. Gunner and I had a talk."

"Are you okay?" I asked.

"Yeah. At least where Gunner is concerned. It's okay. I can't go home, though. Dad met me in the kitchen this morning and I told him not to come to practice today or I'd walk off the field. He demanded to know what my problem was. I stormed out of the house without eating. He didn't show at practice, but he'll be waiting on me at home."

"I'm pulling in the drive now. Come here. Mom will have cooked enough. She always cooks too much. Eat with us and you can do homework in my room. I have to read to Bryony and give her a bath after dinner. Then we can go out and talk on the back porch."

He paused, then I heard him sigh. "Okay. I'll be there in a minute."

*Ain't a Thing Wrong
with That*

CHAPTER 38

BRADY

Gunner hadn't said a word all day. He'd acted normal. It wasn't until after practice that he walked up to me and said, "When are you going to tell me about Riley Young?"

I'd snapped and told him it wasn't his damn business. I had expected a fight then, but he had only agreed that my life was my business, but that if I was hiding her because of him, then we needed to talk.

I let him talk, and he was of the opinion that Rhett wasn't who he'd once thought he was, and even back then it had been hard to believe Riley could be so evil. She had always been honest and nice. If I trusted her, then so did he.

The one thing I had walked away from the talk unsure

of was his asking if Riley might let him meet Bryony. She was his niece, after all, but with all that had happened, that was asking a lot of Riley. I didn't want her to feel threatened in any way.

I told him as much, and he asked that I just talk to Riley about it. I would when I felt like she was ready. Right now, though, wasn't that time. She had to adjust to the fact that Gunner Lawton believed her. I wasn't positive how well that would go over. She had been hurt by him and his family, and if she couldn't forgive him, he'd have to deal with it. He deserved it.

I wasn't sure how comfortable I was going to be at her grandmother's tonight. I didn't know what her parents thought of me and if they'd be okay with me being there, but I wanted to be with Riley.

She was a mom, and she had responsibilities. I was willing to do whatever worked best for her and Bryony. This was it, so I'd be there. If her parents didn't care for me, they'd see I really cared about their daughter and wanted her to be happy. That would hopefully change their minds.

My phone lit up, and it was Willa. I hadn't gotten a call from her in a while.

"Hello," I said, curious.

"Thank you," she said.

"For what exactly?"

"For believing Riley Young. I like her. She didn't deserve what happened with Rhett. I think your believing her helped Gunner let go of his hate. She should get to live in this town, not be ostracized. She took a terrible situation and made the best of it. That little girl is happy and loved. Riley's a good person."

I agreed. Completely. "She's special. I'm the one who should be thankful."

Willa was silent a moment, then said, "Yes, you should be. Tell her I'll see her Friday night. I am saving her a seat beside me."

"I will."

We said our good-byes just as I pulled into the drive at Riley's. I wished that Gunner's acceptance and Riley's chance at a female friendship could fix all my problems. A week ago this would have been all I needed.

Not now. My problems were deeper. Unfixable.

Riley opened the door before I got to it with Bryony at her legs waving at me as I walked toward them. "Mom is setting another place at the table. She's happy you're here. But be ready for Grandmamma. There is no telling what she will say or who she will think you are."

There was a smile on her face as she said it, like she was amused by her grandmother and loved her.

"I'm looking forward to dinner with your family.

Thanks for letting me escape here. Going home seems impossible."

Her smile faded, and she nodded.

"Hi," Bryony said brightly.

I turned my attention to the little girl looking up at me. "Hello, Bryony. Have you had a good day?"

She nodded. "I made corm bwead." I was assuming that was corn bread.

"I can't wait to have some. I'll bet it's delicious."

"Oh, it is. I've already been brought two slices with butter. She keeps feeding me," Riley said with a laugh. "Come on in," she told me as she stepped back so I could enter the house.

Her father was sitting in the recliner with a newspaper in his hands and a pair of glasses perched on his nose. He looked up at me. "Hello, Brady. Glad you could join us tonight. I'm always outnumbered by women."

"Thanks for having me on such short notice," I replied.

He waved a hand as if to say *no problem*. "Not at all. Anytime. We like the company."

"I can't find my yellow butter dish. Have you used it?" Grandmamma asked, shuffling into the room from the kitchen.

"No, ma'am," Riley replied.

She frowned. "I'll need that if I'm gonna make the

rolls for the pot roast." She turned and went back into the kitchen.

"She's been trying to cook all afternoon. Lyla is exhausted from it," Mr. Young said once she was out of the room.

From the little I'd seen, it was like taking care of a child.

"I'll go see if I can help. Brady, do you want to go to my room and start homework until dinner?" She was trying to get me comfortable and not leave me alone with her dad. I appreciated it, but I needed to get in good with her father. I wanted him to approve of me.

"I think I'll visit with your dad and watch the news. See what's happening in sports," I told her.

She didn't hug me, but the expression on her face said she wanted to. Seems my decision had just scored me some points.

"Okay, then. It shouldn't be too much longer," she said before hurrying into the kitchen.

Bryony stayed right behind her, skipping as she went.

"That girl loves her momma. Riley has made a wonderful mom. Couldn't be prouder of her," Mr. Young said as they disappeared into the other room.

"She's really impressive," I agreed.

"That she is. A strong girl. Life hasn't been fair to her, but she seems to find joy in the little things. And, of course, in Bryony. She's the least selfish teenage girl I know."

I nodded.

He set his paper down in his lap and took off his reading glasses, then placed them on the table beside him before leveling me with his gaze.

"You're a good kid. I've always thought so. You've got dreams and talent. Ain't a thing wrong with that. It's admirable," he began, and although that sounded good I was worried about the tone he had taken with me. "But that girl in there is my baby. I've never hurt as badly as I did when her childhood was taken from her. The dreams and hopes for her future were snatched out from under her. It just about broke me. But she showed me and her mother that she's strong and her dreams and hopes could change. With that, so did ours. But her future doesn't fit into your world." He paused and studied me to make sure I was listening.

"I don't want my girl hurt again. She's not had a friend since we left this place. Having you has helped her. I appreciate what you're doing. But don't let her think there could be more for the two of you when there can't be. She's a mother, but she's also just a seventeen-year-old girl."

Hurting her was the last thing I'd ever do. My dreams weren't what they once were either. My father had changed that. I nodded my understanding.

"Yes, sir, the last thing I want is to hurt her. We've talked about the future and where our lives are headed.

She's different from other girls. She more mature and responsible. She cares about things that matter, and honestly, right now I think I need her more than she needs me."

Her father didn't reply right away. He simply sat there and thought about what I'd said. I couldn't promise him we would have it easy. However, I could promise him I'd protect her from me. I would never hurt her. If anyone was hurt when this was over, it would be me.

"Fine, then. Good. I like you, Brady Higgens. I think you're good for each other."

I breathed a little easier.

CHAPTER 39

RILEY

I wrapped the afghan around my shoulders tightly to block the cold night breeze. Brady was beside me on the back porch steps. Dinner had gone well, and Bryony was tucked in bed. She'd enjoyed having a new face around to perform for and entertain.

Between her and Grandmamma, I wasn't sure what Brady thought of my family. Bryony had kept giving him buttered corn bread, which he ate like a champ, Grandmamma had asked him three times what his name was and if he'd seen Thomas, and then to end the night, Bryony had made him a pallet by our bed and told him to stay.

If I sat back and tried to see us through someone else's

eyes, we resembled a zoo. Dad had chuckled through all of it. Mom had kept apologizing under her breath. But Brady had smiled and assured everyone he was having a good time.

"Are you about to vomit from all the corn bread?" I asked him.

"I'm a growing boy. Bryony knows that. She was just making sure I ate enough."

I laughed at that. "Death by corn bread."

"It wasn't bad. I enjoyed it. Was a nice break from my house. This was real. I used to think mine was real, but now that I know what a complete façade it is, I can appreciate the real thing."

"Have you thought about how to handle it? Are you going to confront your dad or tell your mom?"

He sighed and ran a hand through his already messy dark hair. "Yeah, and I don't know. I have to confront him, and I have to tell my mom. Both I need to do. But the idea of how much pain she's going to be in kills me."

I wondered about Maggie. How all this would affect her. She had found happiness in their home. Now this was about to explode.

"Are you going to wait until after the championship?"

He shrugged, then shook his head. "No. I can't. This is more important than football. My mother gets in bed with that asshole every night. Hell, he could be giving her a damn STD."

I hadn't thought of that. But I doubted that would happen.

"She's married, so that's unlikely. It seems to be an affair for both of them."

"She's a whore. She could be having an affair with several men. And I hate to say this, but he could be doing the same. Who's to say she's the only one?"

Good point. I didn't argue that. My stomach twisted at the thought. Just when I thought I couldn't get any sicker.

We sat there awhile staring out at the stars with our thoughts.

Gunner was okay with me and Brady. His girlfriend wanted to be my friend. This should all make me happy. But the way Brady was hurting, nothing could make me happy. His world was being ripped apart. There was nothing I could rejoice over at this point. Nothing that would fix that.

"I'm worried about Maggie. She's just now settling in and living life. She's found security, and I'm about to blow that shit up in her face. With me, I've never had tragedy to face. Life has been easy. So fucking easy I am soft. For Maggie, she's been through so much already. Now the only family she has left is about to explode in front of her. Her mother was my dad's sister, so does that mean she has to go with my dad when he leaves? Because he will leave. My mom won't have to go anywhere. I'll make sure of that. But Maggie should get to stay with my mom. Fuck," he muttered, dropping his head into his hands. "This is so hard. How do I figure out the right thing to do in all this? So many people's lives are going to be affected. Not just mine. How do I protect them?"

He was just seventeen. He shouldn't be having to protect his mother and cousin from this. It was too much responsibility, and it was unfair. I reached over and linked my hand with his. It wasn't much, but it was all I had. In life, sometimes there was nothing that could comfort you. Nothing to take the pain from your chest. But a simple reminder that you weren't alone helped. If just a little.

"Do you think he even considered us for a moment? Me, mom, and Maggie? Or did he just think about himself?"

People were generally selfish. People who cheated on their spouses were the most selfish people I could think of. Yet it happened all the time. It seemed to be the norm now. Maybe we as humans were getting more selfish.

"I think if he'd taken a moment to consider who all he was hurting, he would never have done it."

Brady nodded. "So he's a selfish bastard."

"Yeah," I agreed. Because the truth was the truth.

"I can't remember if football was my dream or my dad's. All I can remember was having a football in my hands since I could walk. But did I choose that or was it forced upon me?"

He was questioning everything now. I didn't blame him. He hated his father because he was hurt. Wanting to rid yourself of everything to do with the person who'd hurt you was common. It made sense.

"Do you love football? Does being on the field fulfill something inside you? Does throwing a pass and seeing it land in the receiver's hands make you feel like you accomplished something?"

He didn't reply right away. I waited in the quiet for him to think about it. Finally he sighed. "Yeah."

That was his answer. "Then it's your dream. No one can take your dream, Brady. They can share it with you or want to be a part of it, but at the end of the day it's yours. You did it. You achieved it. It's yours. No one else can lay claim to it."

He turned his head to look at me. His eyes were almost too pretty under the moonlight. I didn't tell him that, though. I figured he'd take offense to be referred to as *pretty* in any way.

"Can your parents see us?"

I shook my head. "No. Why?"

He leaned in and pressed his lips to mine while his hand cupped my jawline. It was gentle yet took my breath away. I let the cool night air engulf my now-heated body as I leaned into him. His taste was always minty. His lips always soft yet firm. In this moment I wondered where I'd be right now if Brady Higgens hadn't walked back into my life. He was changing me. Teaching me. Opening my world back up.

When he pulled back, it was just a breath of distance. "What would I do without you?" he asked.

I had just been thinking the same thing.

"Fate stepped in and we won't ever have to know the answer to that question."

He grinned and pressed one more kiss to my lips. "I need to send fate a thank-you card. Or a fruit basket," he teased against my cheek as he brushed a kiss there.

Smiling, I wondered why it couldn't be this easy. This simple all the time. Just us. No pain or turmoil. No disaster waiting just ahead. But then it wouldn't be life, would it?

*I Was Convinced She May
Actually Be Perfect*

CHAPTER 40

BRADY

The call I had with my mom last night when I told her I would be sleeping over at Riley's didn't go well. She knew something was wrong. My dad and I had always been close. This rift between us was confusing her, and the more I kept the reasons why inside, the angrier I got. My hate for the man I'd once loved was intensifying.

I didn't sleep well, and when Mrs. Young walked into the living room this morning I was already awake with my history assignment in my lap, working on it.

"You're up early," she said. "I thought with the late night y'all had outside you'd still be sleeping."

"No, ma'am. I needed to get my homework done. I hope we didn't disturb you last night."

"Not at all. It does my heart good to see Riley have someone her age around. She's been without that for so long. Hearing her talk and laugh helps me sleep at night."

The more I heard Riley's parents talk about her, the more I was convinced she may actually be perfect. The girl had to have faults. I just couldn't figure out what they were yet.

"I've got biscuits I made up last night in the freezer I'm about to pop in the oven. Bryony loves honey and biscuits, so I make them once a week as a treat. I can get you some coffee while they're baking."

"Not a coffee drinker, but thank you," I told her.

"That's right. I keep forgetting. What about some milk?"

I set my book down. Didn't feel right having her wait on me. "I'll get it. You just point me to the glasses."

Riley walked into the room just as I stood up. Again her hair was messy from sleep and she looked beautiful.

"You're an early riser today," she said with a sleepy smile.

"So are you," her mother replied.

She shrugged and touched her hip. "My bed buddy kicked me a little too hard in her sleep."

Her mother chuckled and walked into the kitchen. "Come on in. I'm getting the biscuits going before I leave. Grandmamma is still asleep, but I will get her oats cooking too. She will be up any minute saying she's hungry."

Riley yawned and covered it with her hand while she nodded.

"Got it."

Her mother smiled. "You need coffee."

Riley nodded some more. "Yes, I do."

"I'll get the coffee going. You get Brady some milk."

Riley walked over to the cabinet and went to work getting me a glass and pouring me some milk. I decided these women were like my mother and set on serving me. So I let it go.

"Thanks," I told her as she handed it to me.

"You're welcome. Have a seat at the bar. I'll join you in a moment. Soon as I have caffeine."

She made herself busy, and I watched her, forgetting her mother was even in the room. Today she wouldn't get dressed and go to school. No senior-year memories for her. She'd take care of her grandmother and daughter, then do all her schoolwork on a computer. I wanted her to have more than that.

Yet she seemed happy with this.

"Hey, Mommy." Bryony's voice broke into my thoughts and Riley spun around to see her daughter standing there with blond curls sticking up all over the place and a pair of purple pajamas with what looked like a pink pig in a red dress and yellow rain boots all over them.

"Good morning, sunshine. Biscuits are in the oven," she said, bending down to scoop her daughter up and hug her tightly.

She didn't seem sad or like she was missing out on anything. She seemed complete. Happy. No hate or bitterness. She'd been through hell and she'd come out okay. Settled and balanced. That gave me hope. Not only for me but my mom and Maggie.

Riley had been strong. I wanted her strength.

"I want uney," she said, slapping her small hands on each side of Riley's face.

Riley laughed. "I know you want honey."

"Give me kisses, little princess. I have to go to work. Your biscuits will be ready soon," Riley's mother said to Bryony.

Bryony kissed her cheek and patted the other.

"Have a good day, girls. You too, Brady," she called out, then left the kitchen.

Riley put Bryony in her high chair and placed some

raisins on the tray. "I need some coffee. You eat these while we wait on the biscuits," she told her.

Bryony smiled over at me and handed me a raisin in her little hand.

"Thank you," I replied, taking it from her. "I like your pajamas."

She looked down at her clothes. "Peppa," she informed me.

I wasn't sure if Peppa was how she said *pig* or something else, so I just nodded like I understood.

"I wuv muddy pubbles," she added and grinned at me before smashing some raisins in her mouth.

"The translation to that is Peppa Pig is who is on her pajamas and Peppa says *I love muddy puddles* often."

"Geowge," Bryony blurted out.

"She also says 'George' a lot. George is Peppa's little brother."

I wasn't up to date on kids' television. "I guess *Dora the Explorer* and *Bear in the Big Blue House* have retired, then." Those were the shows I remembered being popular when I was a kid.

"Oh no, Dora is still going strong. Bear has left us, though."

The oven dinged and Riley went over and took the biscuits out. "Breakfast is ready."

I enjoyed watching her and Bryony together. Even

when Riley's grandmother came in the room asking about Thomas, the welcoming, happy feeling of this place was one I didn't want to leave. Or was it that I just didn't want to leave Riley? Could it be that wherever she was would feel like home?

Go, Lions!
CHAPTER 41

RILEY

A Lawton Lions football game. Not something I ever planned on attending when I moved back here. All day I had been nervous. It wasn't like I could back out, either. This was for Brady, not me.

If it were for me, I'd be staying here with Bryony watching it on television. Both my parents were so happy I was going, though, it was almost embarrassing. Mom actually offered to take me shopping for something to wear. I assumed jeans and a sweatshirt were just fine. I declined her offer. You would think I was going to prom.

Last night Brady had gone home to sleep. He'd texted me after dinner at his house and said his dad hadn't come home for it. Which made him even angrier, although it had been a meal he could enjoy with his mom and Maggie.

Maggie had also asked him questions after dinner about what was wrong with him. He'd avoided them and locked himself upstairs after helping his mother clean the kitchen. Tonight wasn't going to be easy on him.

Bryony was sitting in my mother's lap watching the six-o'clock news when I walked into the living room.

"You look pretty," Mom said with a pleased smile.

I had changed shirts three times and decided on a thermal dark blue shirt with my brown leather jacket. I wasn't sure what to expect tonight, but my leather jacket gave me some sort of odd comfort. Like a shield or something.

"Mommy cuwls," Bryony said, pointing at my hair.

I had rolled my hair a little with the curling iron. I didn't want to look like I was trying too hard, but I liked it when my hair had some curls in it. I touched them, wrapping a strand around my finger.

"Yes, Mommy has curls tonight. Just like Bryony," I told her, then walked over to kiss her sweet head.

"Thanks for watching her again tonight," I told my mom.

"We are happy to. She's not a problem. Besides, seeing you get out like this does me good."

I had great parents. When life turned on me, they were

there holding me up. They were my support system, and without them I wasn't sure where I'd be.

"I love you," I told her.

"And I love you. No matter how old you get, you're always going to be my little girl. You'll see that one day when this one is a teenager."

I didn't want to think about my baby being all grown-up. I loved having her small hand tucked in mine and her body curled up against me at night. I hadn't thought about how my mother must feel. I did now, though.

"I just hope I'm half as good a mother as you are."

My mom chuckled. "Oh honey, you are already more than that. I couldn't be prouder of you."

Bryony held her little arms up to me. "I wuv you," she said, wanting to join the affection.

I took her from Mom and held her against me. "I love you too."

She squeezed me tightly with her little arms, then I gave her back to my mother. "You two have fun. I'll see you later."

"Go, Lions," Mom cheered.

I just hoped the Lions could pull this off. Brady was carrying the weight of a secret none of them understood. They were all counting on him to pull them through. The fear that he might fail them wasn't even in their thoughts. They all trusted he'd be their star quarterback.

I wasn't worried about the game. I wasn't worried about the championship. I was worried about Brady. This could be asking too much of him.

Parking and walking into the game alone wasn't as intimidating as I had feared it would be. I'd gotten over a lot since the last time I'd walked on this ground. Brady had changed me, helped me. And I hoped I had done the same for him.

I saw people I recognized, and they saw me. Many took a double take like they couldn't believe I had the nerve to be here. I saw more than one jaw drop as I paid my ticket and walked inside the gates.

I wasn't sure how I would find Willa, but I figured I would look for her and then just take a seat if I couldn't see her. I didn't have to sit by her to make it through this game. I just needed to be where Brady could see me. And away from his parents.

"I'm surprised you're here, but then I had faith you'd show." To my left, Willa was walking up to me. She was wearing a Lawton Lions sweatshirt and a pair of jeans. Her blond hair was in a ponytail, and it swayed side to side with each step.

She had been looking for me. That was nice of her.

"I'm definitely here," I agreed, taking a quick glance around and realizing we were drawing attention.

Willa seemed to notice too. "Ignore them. They have nothing better to do. I have us some seats saved."

I fell in step beside her. "Are the seats close to Brady's parents?" I asked.

She frowned and looked toward the stands. "No. . . . Do they need to be?"

"Not at all. Actually it's better that they're not."

Willa glanced at me. "Issues with his parents?"

I wasn't going to explain that to her. "No, but I don't think Brady needs the distraction of me sitting near them. They don't know about us, uh, being friends."

Willa nodded. "*Friends.* That's what you're calling it?"

I wasn't sure what else to call it, really. "I think."

She shrugged. "*Friends* is good. Gunner and I were friends too. Once."

"Hey, Willa," Kimmie said as we passed her, then looked at me like I had three heads. "I don't think Gunner will want you with her."

Willa stopped walking and turned to Kimmie. This wasn't going to be the first confrontation we experienced tonight. I hoped Willa knew this. I didn't want to ruin her night.

"What I do and who I do it with isn't your concern, Kimmie," Willa responded in an icy tone.

Then she started back up walking again without waiting

on a response. Willa seemed all sweet and nice, but man, could she be intense.

"Sorry about her."

"I've known Kimmie since preschool. I expected it from her."

Willa looked at me. "She know about you and Brady being . . . friends?"

I shrugged. "I doubt it."

Willa grinned then. "I'd love to see her face when she hears it."

I didn't know how to respond to that. We walked up the steps to the seats she had reserved, and I was happy to see we weren't too high up. Brady could easily see me. It was just finding me in this crowd that would take some time.

My stomach was in a nervous knot as the players warmed up on the field. Tonight would be the hardest one yet for Brady.

CHAPTER 42

BRADY

Seeing Riley in the stands wasn't enough to keep my father's presence on the sidelines from screwing with me. He had moved to stand with the coaches as if he had the right to. Did he think this would make me play better? That seeing him there was the support I needed?

The pass was incomplete again, and we were out of chances. Defense would step in now and try to recover some momentum for us. I jerked my helmet off and walked over to the water. I was avoiding my father at all costs.

"Brady!" Coach called my name. That was the one voice I couldn't ignore.

I turned to him.

He was stalking toward me. "What the hell is wrong, son? You were off the first part of last week, but that was nothing like this week. You can't complete shit."

I saw my father following him and realized he was going to say something too. I couldn't do this. Not here. He needed to leave.

"At this rate, we won't be able to come back after half-time with a miracle. Where is your head?"

I pointed toward the man coming toward us. "Why is he on the damn field?"

Coach turned to see my father, then back at me with a frown. "Your dad?"

"He doesn't play football; he's not a coach. Do you see anyone else's dad down here? He needs to get the fuck up in the stands, where he belongs."

"Brady!" my father's voice boomed with warning that I rarely heard from him.

"Don't you dare correct me, you cheating sack of shit. I don't want you here! I don't need you here! I can't stand the fucking sight of you!" I was screaming now, and some of my teammates could hear me. I just didn't care.

He stilled at my tirade and stared at me in disbelief. Was it because I was yelling at him or because I'd called him a cheater? I wasn't sure.

"You need to leave the field, Boone. There are obviously family issues here, and y'all can get that shit settled off the field. But tonight I need the boy's head in the game. You're affecting it."

"We need to talk about this. You don't know everything," Dad said, his voice lowered.

I took a step toward him and glared at him eye to eye. "I fucking saw you. I. Saw. You. With. Her. Get out of my face. Get off *my field*. And leave."

I waited until he blinked and looked away from me. He understood. Without a word he walked past me and toward the exit. I wanted to vomit. Again. Talking to my father like that was hard. Hating him so much was painful. We'd been close my entire life.

This was like ripping off a part of my body and tossing it away. I turned to the stands to see Riley standing up. Her gaze was locked on me, and I could see the concern from here. She looked like she was about to bolt down here. The idea of that actually made me smile. Not a big one, but enough to remind me I wasn't alone. She was there.

"Can you do this?" Coach asked me, bringing me back to the problem at hand.

"I don't know," I told him honestly.

He sighed and ran his hand over his almost-bald head.

"I can't play Hunter yet. He's not ready for this."

They all needed me. This was on my shoulders. It wasn't my dad's dream. It was mine. No one could take my dream or claim it as their own. Riley had taught me that. She was right. I took a deep breath and looked back up at her one more time. I gave her a small nod to let her know I was okay. Then I looked for my mom. My father hadn't gone back to sit by her. She was watching me too. I gave her the same nod, then turned back to my coach.

"I'm ready."

He studied me a moment. "Thank God."

West was waiting for me. He hadn't come over to us, but I knew he'd been watching carefully.

"Something is seriously fucked-up. You gonna be okay?" he said as I stood beside him.

I shrugged. "I can play now. But no, I doubt I'll be okay for a long time."

"This has to do with your dad?"

I just nodded.

"Fuck," he muttered.

"Yeah, fuck," I agreed.

Our defense stopped them from scoring and Gunner's eyes made contact with me. "You good?"

"Enough to win this game," I told him. Then the three

of us jogged out to the field with the others on the offensive line. It was time to score. I had to even the scoreboard before halftime, and I had four minutes and thirty-six seconds to do it in.

"We're running this play," I told West, and he nodded. That meant he was up.

With a quick handoff, I gave West the ball, and he took it and made the first down. Just what I needed. One more of those and I'd pass to Gunner. He could run it in.

And that's exactly what happened.

The crowd cheered just as the last ten seconds ticked away the first half of the game. We had managed to tie it up before halftime.

I glanced up to see Riley's eyes on me. Just looking at her helped. Knowing she was there. I wanted to look at my mom and check on her, but if my father had taken the seat beside her, it would rattle me. I didn't want to see him. I had to get my head clear and ready for the last half.

"What the hell did your dad do to piss you off?" Gunner asked as we walked into the field house.

"Shut up. Jesus, Gunner," West barked at him in disgust.

I wasn't telling them now. My mother didn't even know yet, but she would. My father would come clean.

Then my family would explode. Nothing was ever going to be the same.

"Let's focus on winning this game first," I told him, then walked ahead of both of them and into the field house, with the familiar smell of sweat, deodorant, and the desire to win.

Back Off, Serena
CHAPTER 43

RILEY

One point. The difference between kicking a field goal or going for two. West had taken the ball and gone for two. In that five seconds, I didn't breathe. I was pretty sure Willa didn't either. The entire Lawton side was on their feet in silence. Not sure what to expect. It was a gamble. Had they just kicked a field goal, it would have tied the game and gone into overtime. But the moment Brady handed West the ball, an audible gasp went through the stands and everyone was on their feet.

Because if West failed, they lost the game. By one point.

West made it through the other team's defensive line and the crowd erupted. I actually sank down and let my heart rate slow. That had been a massive gamble that I couldn't believe they took. But Brady had returned to the field after halftime playing differently. Less methodical and more aggressive. He took several chances. A few didn't work, but this one did.

The team all piled on top of one another as fireworks went off behind us. They were prepared to win this game. They'd even had fireworks set up. I wondered what they would have done had we lost.

"That was insane," Willa said, sitting down beside me.

I just nodded.

She shook her head in disbelief. "They've never been that risky before."

She meant Brady had never been that risky before, but she wasn't going to say it. I understood. She didn't know what was going on tonight. No one did. But they'd all seen Brady pointing and yelling at his father. Then his dad had walked off the field. I'd heard people whispering about it most of the game.

Willa never asked me or mentioned it, though. I was thankful for that. She seemed to know something was wrong but it was a secret.

"The boys will be a bit in the field house. We can wait until the crowd clears some before we walk down there."

I wasn't completely sure I was supposed to wait on

Brady. He had his family to deal with now. I knew his mom would have questions.

"The field party will be crazy tonight. Your first one back should be one to remember, at least."

I hadn't thought about that. The field party was always after the game.

Going to the field party didn't seem like something Brady was going to be up for tonight. But then I wasn't sure what had actually been said on that field, so maybe he wanted to go blow off steam.

"Not sure if I'm supposed to be going. Brady hasn't mentioned it."

Willa smirked. "He watched you most of the game. I don't think he's planning on going to the field party without you."

She didn't understand, and I couldn't explain it. So I just smiled.

"We can head down that way if you want. The crowd around the door is getting thick. I didn't think about everyone wanting to congratulate them."

I stood up. "Okay."

Brady's mom was waiting, but his father wasn't around. I was glad he'd at least left. Brady wouldn't want to see him when he got out.

"I'd better call my nonna and give her an update on

where I am and what we are doing. She probably watched the game on television and already knows we won."

Willa's nonna was Ms. Ames. She had been the cook at the Lawton house for as long as I could remember. She made the best chocolate chip cookies. I would always sit and have some with a glass of milk and talk to her in the kitchen when I was dating Gunner.

I watched the door and guys began coming out, but none of them I knew. Younger players who didn't get much playing time came out and hugged family members or kissed girlfriends.

"Why are you here?" Serena's voice was laced with hate.

I didn't look her way. "Waiting on someone."

"You're sitting with Gunner's girlfriend. You're probably the reason they struggled out there tonight. Just because Willa is too dumb to know who you are, Gunner knows. You need to leave. No one wants you here, slut."

I found it ironic that Serena would call anyone a slut. Even more so that it was me, a girl who had sex once in her life, and that had been against my wishes. My screaming and clawing and crying for him to stop had made that clear enough.

But this was what I should have expected. This was what they all thought of me, and walking into it was asking for this. I had to be tough and take it or continue to hide. I was done hiding. I was ready to be tough.

"I'm sorry, I forgot to call you and ask you permission to come tonight. Must have slipped my mind," I replied to her, and again I didn't look her way.

"Back off, Serena," Willa said, stepping between us.

Serena laughed. "You do know who this is you're all buddy-buddy with? Right? Gunner hates her. She ruined his family."

Willa rolled her eyes. "She didn't ruin his family. Jeez, get your story straight. And yes, I know who she is and what she was falsely accused of. No one asked you to come over here. Go talk to someone who likes you."

Willa turned to me. "Ignore her. I always do."

I really liked Willa Ames.

"Gunner isn't going to be happy about this," Serena threw out one more time, then spun to strut away as if she were important.

"She never got better, I see," I said to her retreating back.

"Nope," Willa agreed. "Seems to get worse."

"Thanks," I told her. I didn't have friends a few weeks ago, and now I felt as if I had two.

"Anytime. I've had my own problems with Serena."

I started to say something else when Brady walked out

of the locker room. I didn't go to him. I stayed back and waited on him to see his mother first. She would be worried and need answers. I had no idea what his answers would be.

She walked right up to him and hugged him. I watched as he held her a little tighter than expected and whispered something in her ear. Then his eyes met mine and he motioned for me to come to him with his finger as he held his mom.

"I think you're about to catch up with his mom," Willa said with a smile.

"Yeah, I think so too," I agreed.

"I'll see you later."

"Okay," I replied.

Then I headed over to Brady. And his mother.

I'm Walking My Girl
to Her Car

CHAPTER 44

BRADY

After hugging Mom and telling her I loved her, I pulled back and watched as Riley made her way to me through the crowd. She'd been my lifeline tonight. The one place I could look that was safe. I wanted her to understand that.

"Mom, you remember Riley," I said as Riley came up beside me.

My mother's eyes lit up in surprise as she turned to Riley. "Yes, I do. Hello, Riley. You're just as beautiful as I remember."

Having Riley at my side not only gave me comfort, but it also kept Mom from asking questions about my father's disappearance and what happened on the field.

"Hello, Mrs. Higgens. It's good to see you."

"I've been meaning to call your mother and get together sometime for coffee. I'd love to catch up with her."

"She'd like that. The lemon cake you sent over was delicious. We all fought over the last piece. Bryony won, though."

At Bryony's name I could see mother's confusion.

"Bryony is Riley's daughter," I told her.

"Oh, yes. I hear she is just as beautiful as her mother. I look forward to meeting her. I'll be sure to send another lemon cake over this week. You can tell her it's just for her."

Riley beamed, and I could hug my mother again for that. If anything, my mom was the kindest most thoughtful woman I knew. Making Riley at ease about Bryony and even offering to do something like that made me love her more and hate the man she was married to.

"She'd love that. Thank you," Riley said, still smiling. I had seen the anxiety on her face when she walked up to me and now seeing the relief and happiness there made my heart ache less. Knowing Riley was okay and happy among the people who had once caused her pain helped me heal some. If that made any sense at all.

"Well, I need to get going. Find your dad," Mom said, glancing back at me with unanswered questions in her eyes.

"Do you need a ride?" I asked her.

She looked around as if she wasn't sure before giving me a little shrug. "Maybe."

"I drove. So I need to take my car home anyway. You take your mom home and I'll see you tomorrow?" Riley said that as if it were a question.

"I'll pick you up at your place in thirty minutes," I told her.

"Oh." She glanced at my mother then back at me. "Okay. If that changes, just call. I understand."

I bent down and pressed a kiss to her lips right there in front of everyone. I knew they were all watching us. I knew there were questions. I wanted them answered. They could go home tonight and talk about Brady Higgens kissing Riley Young right there in front of God and everyone and hopefully forget the scene with my father. For my mom's sake, at least.

As for Riley, I wanted them to all know she was with me. We were together. And they could all get the fuck over it.

"After a night like this one I want to be with you. I'll be there in thirty minutes."

She looked up at me wide eyes and nodded, but her attention shifted to something over my shoulder. There was a flash of fear in her eyes. "Okay."

I glanced back to see where her attention had been turned to and saw Gunner approaching us. I was ready for this. In a way I had asked for it by kissing her in public. Gunner was my friend, and I hated all the shit he had been dealt. However, his family and the rest of this town had equally hurt Riley. I wouldn't allow him to embarrass or hurt her any more.

I prepared myself as I positioned my body in front of hers. The time had come for this, and I wouldn't let her down. It was my chance to prove to her just how much she meant to me. This wasn't some high school fling. We were more than that.

"Since you're gonna make out with her in public, I figured I'd come over here and be friendly. So the whole damn field party knows this is good. I'm not hating on Riley or you," Gunner said as he and Willa appeared at my side.

Gunner looked at me but directed his words to Riley. "Glad you came, Riley Young." It was his way of letting me know this was okay with him. Maybe he wasn't giving Riley the apology she deserved, and I hoped one day he would. But for now I could accept this. I still stood partially in front of her because it made me feel safer. Like no one could get too close.

Riley glanced toward Willa, then back to Gunner. "Thanks. Me too."

Gunner turned to my mom. "Gorgeous as always, Mrs. Higgens."

Mom smiled. "Thank you, Gunner. You played an amazing game. You boys never cease to surprise me."

Gunner glanced at me. "Yeah, well, Brady never ceases to surprise me."

I smirked, knowing the last call could have gone badly but I'd run over it with Coach and he'd told me if I could pull it off, then go for it. We'd make the headlines.

"Go big or go home," I told Gunner.

He chuckled. "Yeah. Well, we went big, all right. Can't wait to see what the paper says about it in the morning."

Me either.

"See y'all at the field?" he asked.

I really wanted Riley alone, but I figured we would stop by for the team's sake. "Yeah. We will be there."

Gunner shook his head, smiling. "This year has been full of surprises. I'm almost scared to see what happens next."

I knew what he meant. It had all started with Maggie coming into our family and West losing his dad to cancer. The whole dynamic of things shifted, then West changed. For the better. Then Gunner's family went to hell with secrets no one expected. Now I was dating Riley Young.

I knew what was coming next. The smile left my face. Because what came next was my tragedy. The perfect Higgens home was about to fall apart around us.

I glanced over at my mother. "You ready to go home?" I asked her.

"Yes, but I don't want to rush you."

"I'll see y'all later," I told Gunner and Willa.

Riley said her good-byes to Willa and they whispered about something that made Riley laugh.

"Come on, we will walk you to your car," I told her.

I wasn't letting her face this crowd without me. She was now the center of attention, and I knew she could feel the eyes on her. I had kissed her and Gunner had acted like they were friends. This town was stirring in it.

"You don't have to do that. I can get there okay by myself," Riley said.

She apparently didn't know that the scene we had just given everyone had made her an open target. People would want answers. And they wouldn't come to me to get them. They'd go after Riley. I was going to keep her safe from that.

"I'm walking my girl to her car" was all I said in return.

This Was the Field Party, But After
a Game It Was Brady's Show

CHAPTER 45

RILEY

It was exactly twenty-eight minutes later when Brady pulled up in my drive.

Mom had been waiting on me when I walked inside, and I'd told her about the game although she had watched it. I left out the bit about Brady and his dad. When I told her Brady was coming to get me to take me to the field party, she beamed like I'd just won an award.

I had been worried about leaving them to watch over Bryony longer, although she was asleep and rarely ever woke up at night. Still, she was my responsibility. I didn't like to leave her with my parents too much. Our life had been so different before Brady Higgens had walked back into it. I wasn't used to having anywhere to go.

"I'm so glad things went well. You'll have fun at the field. I remember you always talking about going when you were younger. That got snatched from you," she'd said.

I was coming home from the field party when Rhett had pulled down a dirt road and raped me. That wasn't a fond memory, although the result was my daughter. The moment I held her in my hands, the emotions regarding that night faded. They no longer seemed important. She was all that was important.

Mom was now in her bed, and I locked the door behind me as I stepped outside to meet Brady halfway on the sidewalk. He'd been coming to the door to get me. I liked that about him.

"Everything okay?" I asked him, knowing his mother would have wanted answers once they were alone.

He looked pained. Like the weight of the world was on his shoulders. "No, not really. Doubt it will ever be okay again. She asked and I told her to talk to her husband about it."

"You called him her husband?" I asked

He nodded. "I can't call him anything else. I even hate calling him that."

"Was he at home?"

He shook his head. "No. And when she called him, he didn't answer. My guess is he ran off to tell his girlfriend they were about to be exposed. Fucker left my mother there alone. He didn't even tell her he was leaving. She knows something is very wrong. I can see it in her eyes."

"Should you go home and stay with her? What if he comes home tonight and tells her?"

Brady paused at the passenger side door. "I thought about it. But if he's going to tell her, I don't think she would want me there. That would upset her more for me to hear. I'm not planning on staying out too late, though."

I didn't blame him. His mom was going to need him soon.

He opened the door and I climbed inside.

I watched him walk around the front of the truck, and instead of tonight's victory being a reason to celebrate, it was the furthest thing from his mind. His father had taken that from him too.

We drove in silence toward the field. His hand held mine firmly as if he needed the reassurance that I was there. That he wasn't alone. I thought about his mom and wondered if she was facing his father now or if she had any idea as to what was to come.

When he pulled into the darkness of the trees and toward the light of the bonfire, I remembered a night like this one in August when I had come here. I hadn't planned on getting out. I'd just wanted to see it. See the people here that I had left behind. The only person I saw was Brady, and he glared at me. That one look had told me how unwelcome I was. He hadn't had to say anything.

Now here I sat with my hand in his, in his truck, about to walk into this scene while his world fell apart around him. Life was funny like that. The twists and turns it made were never expected. You couldn't predict this. That made life interesting, worth going on and seeing how it would change.

Brady didn't know that yet. He would find out one day. When this was a memory. The pain would heal. Telling him that didn't help the present, though. So I kept my mouth shut and looked at him as he stared straight ahead. As if getting out of the truck was too much right now.

"They think my life is perfect," he said, watching the people laughing and partying in the distance. "I always had the easy life. All of them have probably faced something. Not me. Not until now."

I didn't have a response for that. I didn't think he needed one. He was lost in his thoughts. I let him collect himself and get mentally ready to act like the Brady Higgens they were all expecting.

This was the field party, but after a game it was Brady's show. They all wanted to be near him. He knew that, and tonight that wasn't going to be easy.

"You ready?" he asked, squeezing my hand.

"If you are," I told him.

A sad smile touched his face. "Then let's go."

We walked toward the party with our hands once again linked. If the kiss wasn't seen by enough people after the game, this would be noticed by the entire crowd here.

"There are West and Gunner. Maggie's there too. You'll like her," he told me. I already did. From what I knew of her.

People shouted out his name, and he waved at them as we went straight to his closest friends. A truck was backed up and the tailgate down. Asa sat on it with a redhead, who looked familiar but I wasn't sure about her name, standing between his legs. West was on a tire beside Maggie, and Gunner was sitting with Willa on a log.

"Finally got here. What'd you do, stop to make out first?" Asa asked with a smirk.

"Shut up," Brady replied.

"Can't believe we pulled that shit off tonight," West said, holding up a red plastic cup toward me. "Thanks for having the balls to do it. We'll be the talk of high school football all week."

"I wasn't the one to run it past the defensive line. That was all you," Brady told him, sitting down on the other end of the tailgate and pulling me with him. I sat down beside him, but he kept our locked hands on his thigh.

"Shit about gave me heart failure," Asa remarked and took a drink of what I assumed was a beer.

"You thirsty?" Willa asked me. "I'm going to go get another water."

I was, but the way Brady was holding on to me I wasn't sure I needed to leave him. "I'm good for now. Thank you, though," I told her.

She glanced at Maggie. "What about you?"

Maggie stood up and followed Willa toward the large coolers over by the main fire.

"You could have gone too if you wanted one," Brady whispered.

I shook my head. I wasn't leaving him. Not tonight.

"I'm okay."

He nodded and gently gave my hand a squeeze. I squeezed back.

I'm Moving Out
CHAPTER 46

BRADY

I would never have made it through that without Riley. Pulling up outside her house, I wanted to go inside with her. Stay with her. Going home and facing reality scared me. My mother could know now. What would that look like?

"Call me if you need me," Riley said when I put the truck in park. "I'll keep my phone by my ear."

I sighed. "I wish I didn't have to face this. But if she knows, she's going to be broken. I can't not go home. And if she doesn't know, he's going to have to tell her. I've told him I know. I can't let this drag out. What if she were to find out another way or, God forbid, walk in like I did and catch them?"

She didn't say anything because she knew I was right. There was nothing to add to that.

"Thanks for being there tonight. At the game and the field."

She gave me a sad smile. "I wish it had been easier for you. Both of them."

I leaned over and pressed a kiss to her lips. Tasting her and being close like this always eased the ache. She filled a piece of me that my father had ripped away. I needed her.

When she had needed someone, no one had been there. That killed me every time I thought of it. She was so giving and kind. She didn't hold grudges or bitterness from what we'd all put her through.

Reluctantly I ended the kiss. I couldn't stay with her all night, as much as I wanted. I had to go home and deal.

"I'll walk you to the door," I told her, and she shook her head.

"No. Go home. You can watch me safely get inside. No reason to walk with me. You have to get home and check on your mom."

Normally I would argue, but tonight she was right. I'd stayed out longer than I should have. I should be at home.

"Good night," I told her, and the words *I love you* almost fell from my tongue. I stopped them before they came out, but they had been there. So easily. So quickly.

Shit.

"Good night," she replied, and I watched silently as she climbed out of my truck and went inside.

Shit. I didn't need to love her. Not now.

On the drive home, the words *I love you* played over and over in my head, keeping me distracted until I pulled in behind my father's truck. He was here. Lights were on downstairs.

I had left Maggie at the field with West, so it would just be us. With the truth.

Taking a deep breath, I steadied myself and headed inside. Each step I took was heavy, full of dread. The dread grew to fury, and by the time I opened the door I wanted nothing more than to see my father walk out of our lives and never come back.

I heard their voices, and although there wasn't screaming or crying there was a heaviness to the tone. I followed the sound and found them in the kitchen sitting across from each other at the wooden farm table.

My mother's eyes were bloodshot from tears that were now dried. She looked stronger than I had expected. Did she know the truth?

"Does she know?" I asked him point-blank, not giving him room to lie.

He could barely look at me. "Yes."

I walked over to her and slid an arm around her shoulders. She reached up and patted my hand. "We need to talk with you," she said, "about how we are going to proceed from here."

This was it. The moment where this family changed. Forever. The sick knot in my stomach returned, and I realized that as angry as I was, this wasn't what I really wanted either. I wanted the man I'd thought my dad was to be that man.

I sat down at a chair closest to Mom and turned my attention to my dad. I wanted him to talk. This was his disaster. She shouldn't be the one explaining anything to me.

"What you saw was a mistake . . . ," he began.

I wasn't about to let the bastard lie.

"You accidentally had your pants down and a naked woman on your office table?" I asked with disgust.

He winced and glanced at my mother. "That's not what I meant. Miranda and I have been working together a lot over the past year. Things got carried away. In marriage sometimes people go through rough patches and it opens the door for this to happen. I made a mistake by allowing it to happen. I was weak and I will never forgive myself for hurting your mother . . . or you."

I let out a hard laugh full of hate. "Jesus, that's the biggest crock of shit I've ever heard. Your life wasn't rough.

She does everything for you. She is what makes this house a home. Her!" I yelled, pointing at my mother. "She's why I'm who I am. Her. All because of her. So this rough patch is your excuse to stick your dick wherever you want."

"Brady." Mom's voice broke, but I could hear the pleading there asking me to stop.

My father sighed and looked at my mother, then back at me. "I'm moving out. You, your mom, and Maggie will stay here, I'll keep the bills paid, and we will decide in the coming weeks where we are going to go next."

"I'm filing for divorce, Boone. I've already told you that," my mother said, her voice harder than I'd thought it would be.

He looked defeated, and I wanted him to look torn apart like I felt, like she felt. Defeat wasn't enough. He needed to feel agony.

"Whatever you want," he finally said.

Mom stood up. "I'm going to my room. You have everything you need out of there, I assume," she said without looking at my father.

"Yes."

She bent down and kissed the top of my head. "Good night," she whispered, then walked out.

My father didn't make a move to leave, so I turned to him. "I'll never forgive you. I hope you die a lonely old man with so much regret and sorrow you can't find happiness. Not even in death. You tore us apart, but we will be okay. You won't. You'll never be okay again." I stood up. "Don't come to my games. Don't come to my practices. Stay away from me. I want nothing to do with you. Enjoy the blond bitch and know she's all you've got. That's if she leaves her husband."

That was it. I couldn't say more. My chest hurt so bad it made it difficult to breathe. I walked out of the kitchen and to my bedroom. I didn't move until I heard the front door close. I walked to the window and watched him toss a duffel bag in his truck, then drive away.

My memories of the life we had lived as a family were no longer comforting. I didn't want to remember anything that man was a part of. It was almost as if my identity had been taken from me. Who I was compared to who I am now.

I sat down and pulled my cell phone from my pocket.

It's done. He's gone, I texted Riley.

Just saying it felt unreal. Like this was a nightmare I'd wake up from soon.

I'm sorry was her response.

So was I. So was I.

Change Is Still Coming

CHAPTER 47

RILEY

I picked up the phone several times to text Brady and check on him. But each time there was no text from him, so I set my phone down and gave him the space he needed. They had a lot to deal with today. I just wished I knew how to help them. But there was nothing I could do.

Mom didn't work today, so I took Bryony and we went to the park, then to the grocery store for her. While Bryony napped, I focused on schoolwork. By the time dinner came and I still hadn't heard from Brady, I was concerned.

"You seem distracted," Mom said over the table.

Bryony was eating her noodles and chicken with her

fingers, and I had been watching her, my mind somewhere else. I turned back to my food and realized I hadn't eaten anything. "Yeah. Brady's dealing with some family stuff," I explained the only way that I could.

"What's going on?"

I sighed, lifting my eyes to meet her gaze. "I can't tell you." I wish I could, though. I needed her advice right now. She would know what I should do.

Mom nodded as if understanding my situation and didn't push me for more. "You haven't talked to him today?"

I shook my head. I knew he had to focus on his family, but I just wanted to know he was okay. If that was even a possibility.

"That game last night caught some footage of him having words with his dad. They cut from the scan fast, but there was a glimpse. The conversation seemed heated."

I had wondered if the television had seen that. If so, this news was going to come out soon with this gossip to go behind it. "Yeah" was all I said.

"You can't help unless you're asked. Just be there when he needs you."

That was what I was trying to do. But it was hard when you heard nothing from him.

"Chick-chick!" Bryony yelled and slapped her tray.

"Looks like someone was hungry," Mom said, reaching over to put more chicken on Bryony's tray.

"Say thank you," I reminded her.

"Tank ooo," she said, then began shoveling the chicken in her mouth.

"She must have played hard at the park," Mom said, smiling as she watched her.

"Oh yes. Always."

We ate a little more in silence. Dad was working on the car and said he'd come eat once he had it fixed. Grandmamma was taking a nap. So it was just us three.

"Grandmamma has a doctor's appointment on Monday. I'll stay home and take her. That should give you extra time to do schoolwork."

"I'm ahead already. At this rate I'll graduate by March."

Mom took a sip of her sweet tea. "You still planning on getting you and Bryony a place of your own somewhere? Or do you think y'all might stay here now that Lawton is accepting you?"

I didn't know. Not anymore.

Leaving here had been all I could think about. Now I wasn't so sure. Brady had changed that. Yes, he'd be leaving soon, but he had managed to make this place feel like home again. Maybe not completely, but enough.

"I'm not sure yet," I told her. "I didn't expect things to

take the turn they did. Gunner talked to me last night. He was nice. Friendly. West was there too, and it was almost if I hadn't left. Except we have all changed. For the better."

Mom smiled. "Age will do that to you. Change is still coming. This is just the beginning."

I was good with the change so far. But change was always scary. The future wasn't always exciting.

My phone lit up at midnight, and the only reason I noticed was because I hadn't been able to sleep worrying about Brady.

Can you come outside?

Finally. A text from him. The fact that it was at midnight would annoy me if I weren't so relieved. It hadn't been a good day for him. That I already knew without talking to him.

I got out of bed and tucked the pillows around Bryony's little body so she wouldn't miss my warmth. Then I slipped on my flip-flops and went quietly down the hall and out of the house.

Brady's truck was parked with his lights off in the driveway. It was cold, and I was wishing I'd grabbed a jacket. Hurrying, I ran out to his truck and climbed inside, glad to find it warm from the heater he'd been running.

"Hey," I said as I shivered.

"Sorry it's so late," he replied. His voice sounded hollow. Much like a little boy who had lost his favorite action figure.

"I wasn't asleep."

He turned to me. "I helped Mom pack Boone's things up today. We put them outside by the garage for him to pick up. His clothes, boots, shaving supplies, the tie I gave him for Christmas when I was ten years old, the book about great dads I gave him for Father's Day when I was thirteen, all of it. Every memory was packed up and taken out of the house. Maggie took down all the family photos he was in and packed them away. I had her put them up in the attic space left in my room. It was a quiet day. We didn't talk much. Just cleared Boone's stuff out like he was dead. In a way he is. The man I knew is gone. In his place is this impostor that I hate."

I thought about how I would feel if that were my dad. If he'd hurt my mother like that. And me. Would I be able to pack him away and send him off? My chest hurt just thinking about it. Even if he did something that horrible I'd love him. I didn't think he could do something to make me hate him like that. Maybe I was wrong.

"She's cried a lot today. She tried to hide it, but she would walk away and close herself off in the bathroom. I could hear her crying. I wanted to put my fist through a wall at the sound of her sobs. Knowing the man she trusted and loved did that to her."

He was worried about his mom. I loved my mom too. Finding her hurt and upset like that would kill me. If I were in his shoes, I might be able to hate what my dad had done. I wasn't sure, and I hoped I never had to find out.

"How are you?" I asked him. He'd told me about his mother, but he hadn't said how he was feeling.

"Broken. Different. He changed me. He changed us all."

I slid over to sit beside him, and this time it was my hand that covered his. "Tonight at dinner we were talking about how things were changing for me here. Mom said with age we change. There is more to come. This isn't a good change or an easy one, but it's part of your life, and you control how it affects you. Your father can't control you."

He flipped his hand over, and his fingers threaded through mine. We sat there, me looking at him and him looking straight ahead out the window, lost in his thoughts. I wondered how Maggie was handling this, but it didn't seem appropriate to ask that. Not now.

"I don't want to go home. It hurts too much. But I can't stay away because they need me there. With Boone gone, I'm the man now. That's a responsibility I wasn't ready for either."

Something else I understood all too well. When Bryony was placed in my arms, I was an adult suddenly. Life turned and I was terrified.

"Those things that terrify us can make us stronger and become something beautiful. When I had Bryony, I was more scared than I'd ever been. She was a living, breathing human and I was in charge of her life. Keeping her alive, taking care of her. In a second my world turned on its axis, and I thought I'd never make it. I would fail. But I didn't. And I wouldn't give her up for the world. The person she made me is strong, brave, and I love who I have become."

He squeezed my hand. "Thank you. I forget when I'm in that house that I'm not the only person on earth to go through something so difficult. I think it's all on me. No one's done it before. But you did something much harder. My mom is an adult and Maggie is seventeen. Taking care of them is nothing like being handed a baby to protect." He paused and looked at me. "If this makes me half the person you are, I'll be thankful. The hate I have may actually fade to disappointment. I want your strength."

He was stronger than he realized. We all were. When faced with something like this, we found the strength inside us that we hadn't needed to use before. It was being brave enough to use it that made the difference. Finding an easy escape or running from it didn't make it go away. Facing it head on, knowing you could withstand it and overcome it, was what made you tough enough to live life.

CHAPTER 48

BRADY

The rest of my weekend I spent taking care of my mom and helping her any way I could during the day. Once I was sure she was asleep at night, I would go to Riley's and we would sit in my truck for hours and talk. Sometimes we would just sit in silence. We didn't need to talk. Just being there with her made it better. She reminded me I was strong enough for this. A fairy-tale life wasn't real for anyone. We all faced something hard.

Monday I didn't want to leave Mom and go to school, but she made me. She said my staying home wasn't good for us. We had to learn to live life regularly again. Seeing her red eyes from crying sliced through me every time

I looked at her. It also made the hate I felt for Boone grow.

No one at school knew what was happening. I didn't want to talk about it. Soon enough the entire town would know. Luckily no one was talking about my fight on the field with Boone. They all were talking about the last play of the game and Riley Young being my date. And, of course, our kiss.

That helped keep my mind off things. But in class, when it was quiet, my thoughts went to my mom and I worried about her. It was just after lunch when Maggie found me in the hall.

"I can't stop worrying about Aunt Coralee. I'm checking out and going to the house. I wanted you to know so that you could stop worrying too. You need to stay here for practice, but I don't. I can miss some classes."

Mom would argue with her that she shouldn't have left school, but I didn't tell her that because I wanted her to go. I didn't want Mom alone.

"Yeah. That would be good," I agreed.

Maggie nodded. "West is letting me take his truck. Give him a ride after practice. He may forget he's without a vehicle."

"I'll take care of him. You go be with Mom."

The look she gave me was a mirror of my own thoughts. We loved her. Watching this was hard for Maggie, too. She'd just found happiness and security, then this happened. I had to remember that Maggie was dealing with this just as much as I was. Possibly more. She'd been through a living hell much worse than this.

"Hey," I said to her as she started to leave. She turned to look back at me. "If you need to talk. Or anything. I'm here. Always."

She gave me a sad smile. "Thanks. We're going to be okay, Brady. All three of us. We can survive this."

She was right. We could.

Practice was grueling. The last play of the game may have been a success, but the fact that we'd had to pull off a miracle to win meant we hadn't played the game like champions. Coach drilled that into our heads a million times in the two hours we were on the field today. There wasn't a part of my body that didn't ache.

Mom would have dinner ready, and going home to eat with her and Maggie was important right now. Problem was I really wanted to see Riley. She was what kept me sane in all this.

I picked up the phone and called Mom.

"Hello." Her voice wasn't the usual cheerful tone I was used to.

"Hey, Mom, how are you?"

She sighed. "Good. Maggie and I cleaned house today,

made cookies, and are finishing up supper. Are you coming home or going to Riley's?"

Maggie had been with her all day. It was my turn to take over and give her a break. I couldn't expect Maggie to take care of my mother all the time, just because this was hard on me.

"I'll be there in a few minutes," I said, almost reluctantly.

Mom paused. "Why don't you invite Riley and Bryony to dinner? I'd love to have them and get to visit with her daughter. Would be good to have a baby around here to lighten things up."

The woman was a mind reader. She knew why I had called and what I was dealing with internally without my saying a word. "Thanks, Mom. That would be great. Let me call her."

There was a soft laugh from her, and hearing her laugh even a little helped.

"I've made plenty tonight."

As soon as I said my good-bye, I called Riley, hoping she hadn't eaten yet and this was a way I'd get to see her.

"Hey," she answered after the first ring.

"Have you eaten dinner?" I asked her immediately in case she was in the middle of it. I wasn't above begging her to stop midbite and come with me.

"Uh, no, Mom was waiting on Dad."

"Good, because Mom has invited you and Bryony for

dinner. She said it would be good to have a baby around to lighten things up." *And I want to see you really damn bad. I didn't add that last part.*

"Oh," she said, then paused. I was afraid she was thinking of ways to turn my offer down, so I dove right back in.

"I missed you today. I want to see you, but I need to go home to Mom, too. If you'd come, that would make this easier."

Yes, I just threw in the *feel bad for me* card. I wasn't ashamed of it. I was a desperate man who was in love with a girl and couldn't admit it because what he had seen of love sucked in the end.

"Okay. Yes, we'd like that. Bryony will think this is an adventure. She's not used to going somewhere new. When do we need to come over?"

I let out a sigh of relief. She was coming, and dinner wouldn't be so hard now. We would all have something else to focus on other than Boone not being there. And why.

"I can come get you," I told her, turning my truck down her road.

"Okay, but we will need to move Bryony's car seat to your truck."

"I'll do it as soon as I get there. Y'all just get ready."

It was funny how the idea of eating dinner with Riley and Bryony at my house made things feel lighter. Happier.

It All Seemed Normal
CHAPTER 49

RILEY

Brady's house was like I remembered. But this time I was walking in as a mother, and his . . . friend who was a girl. I had no idea what to call us, really. Asking him to make that clear while his life was in turmoil was inappropriate. So for now we were friends, I guessed.

Brady led us to the kitchen, where the smell of fried chicken permeated the air. Bryony was holding on to me tightly. She wasn't used to new places. We had our routine, and we had just stepped out of it. As excited as she had been when I told her what we were doing, she was nervous now.

"Hey, Mom, we're here," Brady called out just before

he walked into the kitchen. I followed behind him with Bryony on my hip.

His mother was wearing a pink-and-white polka-dot apron and holding a cast-iron skillet full of biscuits in her hand when she turned around to greet us.

"Hello." She smiled brightly.

Brady walked over and kissed her cheek and whispered something in her ear. She patted his cheek and then turned to us. "Riley, she is precious," she told me as she set the skillet on the table and made her way over.

"Hello, Bryony. I'm so glad you came to eat with us tonight. I've made cookies for later. Do you like chocolate chip cookies?"

Bryony eased her grip on me and turned to Coralee. She had said the magic words. Cookies. She nodded her head and her blond curls bounced, as did the pink bow I had in her hair.

"Oh, good. I need help eating all those cookies. If it's okay with Mommy, I may send some home with you. Brady can't eat them all."

Coralee had just made a new friend.

"I eat them," Bryony assured her.

That got a laugh out of Coralee, and I could see the tension Brady had been carrying on his shoulders ease. Hearing his mother's laughter was helping him. They both needed this.

"I've got to put butter on the biscuits. They're not hot anymore, just warm. You think you can help me?" she asked Bryony.

Bryony didn't even think about consulting me. She held her arms out to her new friend, and Coralee took her.

"Your mommy will need to bring you over more often. I could use a helper like you."

Bryony glanced back at me as if to make sure I'd heard that. I grinned at her and she smiled back. Her new teeth made that smile even cuter.

"Thank you," Brady said in a whisper as he walked over to me. His hand settled on my hip. "She's not smiled like that since Boone told her."

Bryony had a way of making people smile. Babies really did lighten up a mood.

"Oh, we have new help," Maggie said, walking in behind us.

Bryony looked up at the new person from her place on Coralee's lap as they began buttering biscuits.

"Yes, this is Bryony. She's going to have dinner with us, then help eat those cookies we made today," Coralee said.

"Oh, good. We need another cookie eater." Maggie smiled.

That endeared Maggie to Bryony immediately. Anyone who was on board with her eating cookies was a winner in her book.

"I'll put ice in the glasses. What would you like to drink, Riley?" Maggie asked me.

"Ice water is fine. Thank you. Can I help with anything?"

Coralee looked up from the biscuits. "We have it all done. Bryony is finishing things up. Go ahead and make yourself comfortable. Brady can fix you something to drink, and what can we get Bryony?"

I set the diaper bag on my arm down and pulled out her sippy cup of milk. "We came prepared," I told her, setting the sippy cup down beside my plate.

Coralee frowned. "We don't have a high chair, but I did find Brady's booster seat in the garage. I wiped it down and put it in the seat to your left. Will that work?"

"You still have my booster seat?" Brady asked, sounding amused.

"And your snuggle bear, and your blankie, and your favorite bippy," she replied with a smirk.

"Bippy," Maggie said with a laugh.

Brady rolled his eyes. "Please, God, don't tell West about this."

Maggie turned around and beamed at him. "Me? Never," she drawled.

"What is a bippy exactly?" I asked, curious. I understood Coralee keeping everything. I would too. I planned on keeping every single memory I could of Bryony's.

"A pacifier," she told me. "He called it a pippy at first, then it became a bippy."

"Mom, please," he said, as if begging for her to stop.

She smiled up at him, then turned her attention back to Bryony. "Looks like we are all finished. Let's wash our hands and get ready for dinner."

Bryony held her buttery hands up. "And cookies," she added.

"Yes, and cookies. But first you have to eat some chicken, black-eyed peas, and mashed potatoes."

Bryony nodded ready to agree to anything at this point. Cookies were her ultimate goal.

Brady set my water down in front of me, then put his tea at the place on my right. Coralee settled Bryony down in the booster seat to my left, and Bryony looked over at me like this was the best thing ever. She hadn't sat in a real chair before. Maybe I should get her a booster seat for the house. The excitement on her face at sitting at the table with us was obvious.

Maggie and Coralee set the food in the middle of the long wooden farm-style table. "Help yourself. Y'all let Riley get Bryony's plate fixed first."

I quickly put some of everything in small portions onto

the plastic plate Coralee had set out for Bryony, then began to cut it up into small pieces while the others began to fix their plates.

"Do you like everything?" Brady asked.

I nodded, and he began to fix my plate too. It all seemed normal. Real. And something I could never have imagined in a million years.

*We Didn't Have to Figure
It All Out Right Now*

CHAPTER 50

BRADY

Dinner with Riley and Bryony was just a couple hours, but it seemed to help us heal. Odd how that happens. A reminder of someone else's beauty after pain seemed to do that. Mom cried less. I was able to focus more that week on practice. Maggie didn't leave school early anymore. But twice this week she had gotten home to find Riley and Bryony at my house entertaining my mom.

I knew why Riley was going over there, and if I hadn't already known I loved her, that would have made me love her. I just wished I had more faith in love. And forever.

Riley would be here or wherever she planned on going next year, and I would be at college. Away. Missing her.

"So are you dating Riley Young?" Ivy caught me when I was walking out to my truck Friday. Today was the big game. The end. So they let school out at twelve for students to travel the two hours away to where the game was taking place.

"Yes," I replied, knowing she had seen or already knew about the kiss. Not to mention the field party.

"When did that start? Last thing I heard she had fucked someone and tried to pin the baby on Rhett. Gunner just decided to forgive that cause his brother got drunk and came to homecoming."

Ivy was being catty because she was upset. I had broken things off with her, but that wasn't enough. She had been expecting we would end up together. I knew she planned on following me to college. Not something I wanted or had asked of her. Ever.

"None of that is your business," I told her, jerking my truck door open and tossing my bag inside.

"We were together for eighteen months, Brady. We had taken a break only three weeks and four days before you were seen kissing her. How do you think that makes me feel? It was just a break!"

I had too much to deal with to add this drama to it. "It

wasn't a break. I told you we were over. It was done. We had grown apart and I needed to focus on my future. You wanted things I didn't."

She let out a loud, angry laugh. "That is a break!"

"A breakup," I corrected, then climbed into my truck.

"You pretend to be this nice guy. The good guy everyone wants to be around. Mr. Quarterback with the perfect life. But you are cruel! Selfish! And I am glad to be rid of you! I deserve more than this."

Her ranting was a time bomb that had been ticking. I was glad it was happening and we could move on.

"Okay" was all I said, hoping I could close the door and leave.

"Why Riley Young? She has a baby, for God's sake!"

Because she was my fit. And I loved her. I didn't say that, though. I wasn't telling anyone before I told Riley.

"Good-bye, Ivy" was my response instead, then I closed my truck door and made sure not to hit her before pulling out of the parking spot and heading home to get ready for the last game of my high school career.

Riley's red Mustang was in my drive when I pulled in. It made me smile to see it there. My conversation or assault from Ivy, whatever you wanted to call it, was over. I was home now. Riley was here. I was okay.

I walked in the front door and heard Bryony's laughter coming from the living room.

I went toward the noise to find Bryony at the coffee table with homemade play dough—something my mother loved to do with me as a child. Riley was on the other side helping her roll it into small balls, and my mother was beside Bryony on her knees with a smile on her face again.

The ache my father's departure had caused eased when my mom smiled like that. Her eyes weren't bloodshot from tears today. It looked as if she hadn't cried at all. She lifted her gaze to meet mine. "Look who came to play today," she said, sounding as happy about it as she looked.

I bent down beside Riley. "And y'all made play dough. I used to love doing this."

"And you loved eating it," my mother added.

Riley chuckled beside me, and I cut my eyes over at her. She was beautiful. Her hair was up on top of her head in a messy bun, and she wasn't wearing any makeup. She had the same happy expression my mother did, and sitting here like this with her, spending time with my mom, made me want to kiss her until we both ran out of breath.

"Hey," I said instead.

She blushed as if she knew what I was thinking. I hoped so. "Hey" was her simple response.

"Bryony and I need to finish making the Christmas

tree out of play dough. Riley, would you help Brady get his things together for me? He needs to be back at the school soon to get on the bus."

That was Mom's way of giving us privacy but reminding us not to take too much privacy.

Riley nodded. "Yes, of course."

We stood up and Bryony seemed too preoccupied to care about our departure. I waited until we hit the stairs to press a quick kiss to her lips. I couldn't wait much longer.

She kissed me back, then pushed me gently away. "Someone could see us."

I wasn't real concerned, but she was, so I hurried us along to my room in the attic. There, no one would see us. And I could have my alone time with her.

When we stepped inside, I closed the door before leading her up the stairs to the loft we had fixed up in the attic when Maggie had moved in. She had taken my room and I had finally gotten this room, like I'd wanted for years.

"Thanks for coming here today, spending time with Mom," I told her, putting both my hands on her hips and pulling her closer to me. "She really enjoys Bryony."

"Bryony enjoys coming over here," she replied with a whisper just before I covered her lips with mine.

Kissing Riley seemed to get better every time. She was

always sweet and soft. I wanted to hold her like she was delicate, yet I couldn't seem to get close enough to her. This was when I felt completely whole. Not broken or hurt. With her in my arms, my life was right.

That was love. I knew that now, but it didn't mean love wouldn't end. Even knowing that, I never wanted to end this with Riley.

Her hands slid up my arms, and I shivered from the touch. Wrapping my arms around her, I held her to me as close as she could fit. The feel of her breasts pressed against my chest sent desire coursing through me that I was afraid of acting on.

Most girls that I had dated moved easily, but Riley had been hurt sexually, and I was afraid too much would terrify her. So I held back, and it took every ounce of willpower I had.

She moved up so that her breasts brushed against me and a small moan escaped her. Mary mother of Jesus, I was a saint. I swore to God I'd better get rewarded for this one day. Picking her up and taking her over to my bed was all I could think about.

My hands brushed her bare waist as her shirt lifted, and she shivered this time. So I let them travel higher and she lifted her arms to wrap around my neck, giving me complete access. Or at least it felt that way.

When my thumbs brushed under the wire of her bra

and she continued to kiss me and cling to me, I continued on until my palms covered the soft bare flesh that sent both our heart rates into a frenzy. Her breathing intensified and she began to pant as she held on to my shoulders as if she might fall.

This was more than I couldn't imagine with anyone else ever. Just her. I broke the kiss so I could catch my breath as my hands continued caressing the tender flesh that had hardened under my touch.

"I love you," I told her. The words were out before I could think it through. In this moment we were enclosed in our own little world. Safe from others and the shit life threw at us.

She didn't reply right away, but her eyes closed and she rested her forehead on my shoulder. I slipped my hands around to her back and held her against me. We stood like that while our breathing slowed and the heat from our bodies mingled to make us feel like one instead of two.

This was where I wanted to be. Nowhere else had ever felt this right. No one else would make me feel like Riley Young did.

Brave. Strong. And able to take on the world.

"I love you too. But it scares me," she finally said, breaking the silence around us.

She didn't scare easily. But I understood her fears. I had them too.

We didn't have to figure it all out right now. Or even tomorrow. We had time. And there had to be an answer to this. Because without Riley I wasn't whole.

I've Already Lived Through
a Nightmare
CHAPTER 51

RILEY

Instead of sitting far away from Brady's family this week, I sat beside his mother, and Maggie and Willa joined us. We were all wearing Lawton Lions blue. Brady had actually given me his home jersey to wear tonight. It was huge on me, but Willa and Maggie had on Gunner's and West's, so I didn't feel silly.

The crowd was roaring with excitement, and I was immersed in the smell of popcorn and hot dogs. Tonight was more exciting than last week. This was it. The end and their chance to win the State title. I wanted that for all of them, but I really wanted it for Brady.

I kept scanning the crowd for his father. I knew he

had told his father he didn't want him there, but I was worried he may show up anyway. This was the biggest game in Brady's life so far. I knew his father would want to be here. Not that he deserved to be here but that he would want to be.

"I'm watching for him too," Maggie whispered in my ear. "If you spot him, tell me quietly and I'll go handle it."

I nodded. Neither of us wanted Coralee to know what we were talking about. She had been excited today. Talking about the game and how hard Brady and the boys had worked to get here.

I hadn't realized they'd all been through so much. West had lost his dad at the first of the football season to cancer, Gunner had found out his father wasn't his father but his brother and in turn lost most of his family, and Brady had caught his father in an affair. Three starting seniors who had grown up playing ball together and building dreams all faced something hard, yet here they stood, about to play for the state championship.

I wanted it for them. So did the rest of this crowd. Cowbells were being rung. Cheerleaders were already starting up, and banners were everywhere. I tried not to let it get to me when I saw signs in the crowd that said I LOVE HIGGENS, BRADY HIGGENS IS MY HERO, and the worst one yet: MARRY ME BRADY.

I figured this was just the beginning of all that. He'd be playing for an SEC crowd next year and the female adoration would increase. Yet today . . . he'd told me he loved me.

My heart fluttered in my chest at the memory, and I wanted that. I wanted Brady. What we could have. But winter was almost here. Soon spring would come, and then with its end he would graduate and things would change once again.

"I'm not sure my nerves can handle this," Willa said, looking over at us nervously. "And to think two months ago I didn't care a thing about football."

Maggie laughed. "I know what you mean."

The three of us had changed too. Each for different reasons. Maggie and Willa had also fallen in love, but they had plans. They would go to college with their boyfriends. Build their life together. They didn't have a daughter that came first before anything else.

It made falling in love much more complicated for me. I had been trying to protect myself, and my heart had just gone on ahead and done what it pleased. But then, Brady Higgens was hard not to love. He made it just about impossible.

Coralee reached over and squeezed my hand. "He's looking for you," she said.

I turned my attention to the field and Brady was there staring up at us. I waved and he blew me a kiss before running to the field house with the rest of the team. Warm-ups were over. This would all be starting soon.

"I like you so much more than Ivy," Maggie said. "I did like the brownies, but they did not make up for her endless pointless chatter about stupid things."

Smiling, I wrapped my arms around myself as if to keep warm from the cold wind, when I was actually holding in the warmth that being accepted created inside me. I hadn't expected acceptance here, yet I was getting it. All because Brady Higgens had chosen to believe me. He held a power that most didn't have and he'd used his power for good. In my world, that made him a superhero. If this town had one, it would be Brady.

Not because he was a star quarterback but because his heart was big. He wasn't perfect, and he had made mistakes, but at the end of the day if he had to make a choice, he tried his best to make the right one. Even if it hurt to do it. That was superhero status in my book.

"Not sure what he'd have done without you through all this," Coralee said beside me, her voice laced with emotion. "For him to see what he did and deal with it through the toughest two games of his high school career seems impossible. Him having you has made the difference. You give him strength. I have seen it this week."

I didn't think I'd given him anything but an ear and some advice. Because I knew what having your world fall apart felt like. Brady was strong before I came along. But if I had any part in his making it through all this, then maybe I was a superhero too. Smiling, I reached for my soda and took a sip.

"Ivy seems to have a new interest," Willa said, pointing to the field at the sign Ivy was holding up: GET US STATE, RYKER!

I wondered if Ryker knew he was next for her. Maybe he wanted to be. She was beautiful, and she was the head cheerleader. Ivy had always been the good girl and a little overly sweet. But if she was moving on, then I was happy for her.

"Anyone want a hot dog? The smell is getting to me," Maggie said, standing up.

"I do," Coralee said.

I did too. I stood up. "I'll go with you."

Willa shook her head. "No, thanks. Too nervous to eat."

"Want another drink?" Maggie asked her.

"I'm good for now."

We headed down the stairs and toward the concession stand. It seemed all very normal, like I belonged here. I guessed I did now. Actually I always had. Just because others hadn't accepted me hadn't made me less of a person.

"I know Brady has already said this, but thanks for this week. Your bringing Bryony to visit has helped Aunt Coralee."

I wondered if anyone had asked Maggie how she was doing. "How have you been through all this?"

She shrugged. "I don't know. He's my uncle, but until I moved here I didn't know him that well. I spent more time with Aunt Coralee than with him. Now I know why he was rarely home." She winced. "I'm stronger than Brady because I've already lived through a nightmare."

*Oh God, Save Me from
the Mushy Shit*

CHAPTER 52

BRADY

It was over.

My high school football jersey had seen its last game.

The smell of the fresh-cut grass, the night air cooling my overheated skin.

Next to me, the guys I'd been playing ball with since I was a kid.

This was it. It'd ended, but it wasn't like I had always imagined it would.

West and Gunner were at my side, the crowd's cheering was loud enough to be heard for miles, and the victory we had always planned on was in our hands.

But I wouldn't be celebrating with my father tonight, or any night.

He wouldn't be there when I walked off this field. He wouldn't share in the end of an era. We wouldn't hug and he wouldn't slap my back and tell me good game. We wouldn't rejoice in the three touchdowns that had made us winners tonight.

He wasn't even here. Because he'd made a choice to rip us apart. He wasn't the man I'd thought he was. With tonight's dream coming true, another one was dead.

I didn't have a father to be proud of. I looked to West at my left and thought about how he felt right now. His dad would be thrilled. I knew he was wishing he could be here now. That he had been able to live to see this night.

Then I turned to Gunner, who had never really had a father. He had lived a life of the wealthy rich kid who no one gave any attention to. All along chasing his own dreams. We were all three fatherless now for different reasons, but through it we had become men.

"We did it," West said as we watched the rest of the team jump all over one another and pour the Gatorade over Coach's head in celebration. I always thought it would be the three of us doing that. It was the younger guys, though. The ones who had their own dreams to chase.

"What happens now?" Gunner asked what we were all thinking in some form or another.

"We live life," I replied.

That was the only answer I had.

"I wouldn't have been able to do this with anyone else. We have memories that can't be replaced out here."

I guess all guys go through a form of nostalgia in their life. Ours was happening right there on the field we had snuck out to when we were kids and dreamed about this night. All those plans and dreams had happened, just not the exact way we imagined they would.

"I'm guessing you won't be marrying Selena Gomez now." West smirked, looking over at me. That had been one of my dreams after winning State back when I was in middle school and we planned this night.

"Yeah, I've moved on from Selena. Not my type."

Gunner chuckled. "Damn, we've changed a lot since then."

Yes, we had.

"You gonna tell us why Boone wasn't here and what happened last week?" Gunner asked. I'd expected this question. At least from these two. They'd noticed.

They were my two best friends. I'd been through life with them. We had grown together and watched one another take turns and face tragedy. It was time I told them the truth.

"Caught him with another woman. He told Mom last week after I confronted him, and he moved out this weekend. I don't want to see him," I said matter-of-factly. The emotion behind the words was void now. Although the pain still sliced through me.

"Damn," West muttered.

"Fuck," Gunner said at the same time.

Both of those replies were correct. "Yeah," I agreed.

"How's Coralee holding up?" West asked. He loved my mother like his own.

"It's been tough" was all I said.

Gunner put his arm around my shoulders. He didn't say anything. It was his way of letting me know he was there. I wasn't alone.

"Life sure throws you shit," West said, as if he still couldn't believe it.

It did. But it also threw you good things. Like friends, football, and someone to love you and show you the way to heal.

Glancing over to the stands, I saw Riley with Maggie and Willa. They were all watching us and waiting. They weren't rushing the field like the others. It was our time, and they knew we needed it. This year was halfway over. We would all graduate and move on in a few short months. But we had been lucky enough to find a reason to fight through the bad and come out on the other side.

"Last postgame field party. The night's not over yet," West said with a smile.

It was a two-hour drive back, and we'd all be exhausted when we returned, but tonight we had one last memory to make. There would never be another postgame field party for the three of us. The others had more time. It wasn't ending for them. They weren't moving on. Next year there would be new seniors. Asa, Ryker, and Nash would be the ones leading this team. They would still have the field party, and their lives would be here in Lawton.

Our era was over, and I once thought I'd be sad when it finally happened. Part of me hated to see it go, but the other part knew I had a world out there waiting on me. More memories to make and more dreams to chase.

Turning my attention back to Riley, I knew that she was in that future. I just had to figure out how to make it work and convince her it would. She was made for me. And now that I had her I wasn't going to lose her.

"Does next year scare the shit out of you?" Gunner asked.

"Yeah," both West and I said in unison.

We all laughed and I motioned my head toward the

girls. "But we have them. And I don't know about y'all, but if I can be promised Riley will stay with me through it all, I'm not nearly as scared."

Gunner stopped walking, "Shit. You're already in love."

I held her gaze. "She's really easy to love."

West groaned. "Oh God, save me from the mushy shit."

I slapped the back of his head. "Don't act like you've not been mushy before. And I had to watch it happen with my cousin."

"He's got a point," Gunner agreed.

We walked toward the girls and they entered the gate and met us halfway. This was a much better dream than the one I'd come up with when we were twelve. Much better.

It Was a Part of My Story
CHAPTER 53

Four months later . . .

RILEY

Spring break hadn't been a week for me and Brady to spend together. It had been a week for him to go to the University of Alabama and be given a tour of the college he would be attending the next four—or five years, if he got redshirted. I was happy for him, and watching his dream come true was amazing, yet it meant he was closer to leaving me. Leaving Lawton. His life would change.

So would mine.

I had finished my online high school career two weeks ago, and I was applying for jobs in Nashville. It was only a one-hour drive, and until I could afford a place for me and

Bryony to live, I was going to pay a sitter here in Lawton and work in Nashville while attending Nashville State Community College. They offered many online classes, so with my parents' help I could make it work with Bryony.

Talking about all this with Brady hadn't really come up. Christmas had been difficult for him because of his father's absence. In late January he had agreed to have dinner with his father, and although he wasn't forgiving his dad he agreed to once-a-month dinners. Nothing more.

The divorce was final at the first of this month. That had been another hard time for Brady and his mom. It had been the real end.

With all that going on in his life, I didn't want to bring up my plans. They would just remind us that our time was coming to a close. June would roll around and he'd be leaving at the end of it for Tuscaloosa. I would then begin preparing my new life. My new job, whatever it may be.

I had applied as a bank teller, as a receptionist for several lawyers' and doctors' offices, and I had also applied for a job at the Nashville State Community College library. It would give me a discount on my tuition if I got that job that would make up for the fact that it was less pay.

Waiting to get a job was the hard part. I had two interviews next week. One with a family law office and another with a pediatrician's office. My parents were being very supportive and helpful. They even offered to pay half the day-care costs for Bryony. She was going to love being with other kids during the day. Reminding myself of that was the only way I could handle the idea of being away from her all day.

All of this was something I needed to talk to Brady about. He was coming home tonight. He was planning on me and Bryony eating dinner with him, his mom, and Maggie. Bryony loved going to see Ms. Coralee. She was already asking me when we would go over there.

I was ready to see Brady. I'd missed him this week, but the absence had just been a taste of what was to come. He talked as if we would stay together when he left. But I knew that wasn't going to happen. I couldn't do that. It would hurt too much. Being with him made me happy. However, lately I stayed sad thinking of the future.

I didn't want to live sad. Breaking it off and moving on was the only way I would be able to heal and find happiness. Telling Brady that, however, seemed more difficult with each passing day. He'd texted me about the campus and how awesome it was. He called me every night to talk about next year and the things he couldn't wait to show me.

In his head we would work long-distance. I would come visit when I could and our phone calls would be enough. Maybe his heart didn't ache being apart from me.

With all the excitement of the new college and the legend-ary football team he was going to be a part of, I tried to understand him.

It didn't make my heart hurt less.

When I thought about life without him I would take Bryony on a walk and enjoy her. It reminded me I was a mom and I had a beautiful daughter. Feeling sorry for myself was stupid and shallow.

I glanced down at Bryony as we strolled out of the park, and her eyelids were already growing heavy. She'd played hard today. There had been several kids out enjoying the sunshine. The more she had to play with, the better, as far as she was concerned.

"Riley." A familiar voice said my name. The timbre and who it belonged to registered in my head, but with it came panic. Something I hadn't felt in a while. Something I never wanted to feel again.

I inhaled sharply and reminded myself that I was strong. I wasn't defenseless anymore. I'd known this day would come eventually. But that didn't prepare me for it actually happening.

Lifting my gaze, I met the steel-blue eyes that were shaped so much like my daughter's. The way his eyebrows arched and even the form of his nose looked like hers. Breathing was becoming difficult.

"Is this her?" he asked.

What did *her* mean exactly? Was this the daughter he'd given me unintentionally? The child he claimed wasn't his?

"This is my daughter," I stated with firm authority. There would be no question as to who she belonged to. She was mine.

"Gunner told me she looked like me," Rhett Lawton said as he stared down at Bryony, who had thankfully fallen asleep. I didn't want her to see him or remember him.

I liked Gunner, but at that moment I was not liking him very much. I trusted him and allowed him around Bryony. However, Rhett was out of the question. He was evil, and I wanted no evil touching my daughter. She was nothing like him. Her heart was pure.

"When was she born?" he asked, still studying her sleeping form.

"Why?" I spat back. I wanted him to leave me alone. Leave us alone. Lawton had become a welcoming safe place for us. With Rhett here that changed. He wasn't safe.

"She's mine, Riley. We both know it. I always knew it."

Anger boiled in my veins, and I wanted to grab the nearest rock and hurl it at his head. She wasn't his. "She is mine," I repeated. *"Mine."*

He sighed and for a second he resembled Gunner. Someone who I trusted. Rhett wasn't to be trusted.

"I fucked up. I've fucked up a lot. But I was young and scared out of my mind."

I laughed then. It sounded a bit crazy. Like the laugh you hear from insane people. But his words were insane, so my manic laughter fit the situation.

"You were young? Scared?" I repeated the words like they tasted sour on my tongue. "Really? Well, boo-fucking-hoo. I was fifteen and pregnant from a rape that the father claimed didn't happen. I was a virgin, Rhett, or were you so drunk you didn't notice? You took my innocence, left me pregnant, then turned the entire town against me. My family had to leave here because of you. You almost destroyed me." I paused. "But you didn't. She saved me."

He didn't seem remorseful, just guilty. Like he knew what he had done was wrong, but he wasn't going to be able to change it, so he wouldn't focus on it too much. "You came back; they accept you now. My reputation isn't that great here. In the end, you won."

I was ready to hurl more angry words at him until that last sentence.

I won.

In the end, I had won.

I had a beautiful daughter I couldn't live without. My family never left my side. I had friends who cared about me and were a part of my life and Bryony's. And for now I had Brady.

Rhett had nothing.

"They say karma is a bitch" was my response to that. Maybe it was cold, knowing that his world had also exploded this past year. But I wasn't ready to accept him. I doubted I ever would be. But I could forgive him.

"I don't want you in my life and especially not in Bryony's. The story of her conception isn't anything she ever has to know. But for what it is worth, I forgive you. I will never forget, but I will forgive. Because in the end I was given Bryony."

He didn't respond at first, but he finally nodded. "I just wanted to see her, Riley. I wasn't trying to be a part of her life. I don't want to be a father. I have no example and I would suck at it. But I did want to see her and know what happened . . . what I did . . . all ended okay."

I could tell him that what he'd done had almost ruined me. I had lived in so much pain and anger that I had to see counseling. But none of that mattered now. It was a part of my story. It was a part of me.

"It did," I replied.

He looked back down at Bryony one last time. "I hope she has a good life."

"She will have the best life I can give her."

He nodded, then turned and walked away.

It was as if a chapter had closed in my life. The spring breeze brushed my hair across my face, similar to that of a page turning. I exhaled, then took a step forward, ready for the next chapter life had for us.

*What the Hell Would I Do
without Her?*

CHAPTER 54

BRADY

Riley had seemed different all evening. It had been hard to
concentrate on the questions my mother asked and listen to
the things I had missed here with Riley being quieter than
usual and almost standoffish.

Something was wrong, and I was ready to get her
alone and figure out what it was. Maggie had left to go to
West's house to watch a movie, and Mom was playing with
Bryony in the living room. She had bought Bryony several
toys for our house. The blocks seemed to be her favorite. I
could hear Mom suggesting they build a castle.

"Come with me," I told Riley, taking her hand and

leading her out to the backyard so Mom wouldn't get all weird about us staying too long up in my room.

She went with me easily and without question. Once I had her outside and away from the house, I turned to look at her. "What's wrong?"

I had missed her something fierce this week. Being at Alabama was fun and exciting, but I wanted her there beside me. I wasn't going to be able to stay away from her . . . and Bryony. I missed her too. I realized, being gone, that they had become part of my family. The most important part.

I had asked about football players who had kids and how that worked. If they had special housing, even if I wasn't married. They did. If I had a girlfriend and a child, they could put me in family housing. Convincing Riley of that, though, was going to be difficult.

"I saw Rhett today," she said, snapping me out of my thoughts.

"Did he come to your house?" I asked, feeling a surge of protectiveness. He was going near what was mine. He had no claim to them.

"No, we saw him on our way home from the park. Or I saw him. Bryony was asleep, thankfully. He just wanted to see her. Nothing more. I almost . . . *almost* felt sorry for him."

I hadn't seen Rhett since homecoming, and I didn't care if I ever saw him again. But hearing her say she felt sorry for him made me wonder how he was. His parents' lies had affected him just like they had affected Gunner.

"Is that why you seem distant tonight? Did he upset you?"

She looked away from me, then her shoulders lifted and fell with a sigh.

"I wanted to wait until closer to graduation to talk about this. You still have almost two months of school left. No reason to deal with the future just yet."

But it was obviously bothering her. My being gone to Alabama all week had reminded her that things would change soon. Until I had spent a week away from her and Bryony, I hadn't thought it through. Being apart from them had made me think. She must have gone through the same thing.

"I think we should talk about it now. We need to plan, and I have an idea. I spoke with my representative there, and they have family housing. You being my girlfriend and Bryony being my child, we qualify for a place in family housing. I don't have to stay in a dorm room. Y'all can come with me." Saying it took a weight off my shoulders I'd been carrying for months when I thought of leaving her.

Riley pulled her hand out of mine and put some space

between us. I didn't like that response. It wasn't what I had expected. My stomach knotted up as I studied her face.

"What would we do? I have no family there to help me with Bryony. I wouldn't be able to hold a job and pay for day care and go to school without help. I can't just stay at the family housing and wait on you to have time for us. This is your future, Brady. All you've fought for. All you've planned on. And you need to live in a dorm and go out to bars and enjoy being in college. You don't have a child. The fact that you're willing to sacrifice all that for us doesn't mean I will let you. I have plans. Plans that work for us. For me and Bryony."

What plans? We hadn't talked beyond my going to college and them visiting.

"I want you with me," I told her.

A sad smile came and left. "But we can't be. It isn't what's best for any of us."

I started to argue, and she held up her hand to stop me. "I'm getting a job in Nashville. Bryony is going to day care here, and my parents are paying half of it. Nashville State Community College has online courses so I don't have to go to all my classes on campus. For the next two years I'm going to school there, then when Bryony is ready for kindergarten we will make a move. I'll get my teaching degree and find us a house of our own."

I stood there as she built this future without me in it. One where she and Bryony were moving on and leaving me behind. I couldn't find words. It was like being blindsided. I'd thought she wanted to be with me as much as I wanted to be with her. She'd said she loved me. Did love not mean the same thing to her?

"It's what's best for all of us," she said.

"No! It's what's best for you, maybe. But not me. I love you too much to plan a life without you in it. Obviously you don't feel the same way."

She shook her head, her eyes filling with tears, but I was angry, hurt, and my chest felt like it was about to explode. "If you didn't want me, why did you let me love you? I don't fucking trust love. Does it not mean the same to anyone else? Is that it? I'm the idiot?"

"Brady, no!" she said, taking a step toward me. I backed up. It was my time to put distance between us. I couldn't imagine planning my future and leaving her and Bryony out of it. But she had done that easily enough.

"Don't, Riley. Don't. You want me out of your future, fine. I never wanted you out of mine. All damn week I missed you and thought about how I couldn't do life there without you. You are where I get my happy. You. And while I was there trying to figure out how to take you with me, you were here planning me out of your life."

"I was here trying to prepare for what was to come. I can't take Bryony off to a college campus, Brady. Surely you see that. She's secure here. That's not a place for a baby."

Other guys did it all the time. "They have family housing for a reason, Riley! It's obviously done all the damn time." She was using it as an excuse.

The fact was that Riley didn't love me the way I loved her. She'd have destroyed me in the end. If she loved me enough, she'd make it happen. But this was her excuse. Her way out.

What the hell would I do without her?

*He Thinks He Wasn't
Enough for You*

CHAPTER 55

RILEY

I wiped the tears from my face and took a deep breath before going back inside Brady's house to get Bryony. He had turned his back on me and told me to leave. Our conversation was over. We were over.

Coralee frowned when she saw my face, then turned to look outside where we had been for her son.

"Thank you for dinner, but we need to be going," I said, my voice cracking.

"What happened?" she asked me.

I picked up Bryony and put her diaper bag over my arm. "We don't agree on next year. He sees it differently than I do," I explained. My eyes filled with tears again. "I need to go," I said, then hurried for the front door with Bryony on my hip.

I got her buckled into her car seat and headed for home. The tears streamed freely down my face now, and Bryony was unusually quiet. She knew something was wrong, and she wasn't sure what to do. I didn't like to scare her, so I tried to stop, but another sob broke free.

When we pulled into the drive, I dried my face before getting out and knew that my parents would know I had been crying. They'd want answers, and I wasn't ready to give them that yet.

I never imagined it ending like this. But then I'd never imagined the ending. It had hurt too much to think about.

Bryony patted my face with her little hands as if to console me. I squeezed her tightly against my chest and told her I was fine.

When I walked inside, my mom looked up from the crossword puzzle she was doing on the sofa and an immediate frown crossed her face.

"What happened?"

"Mommy sad," Bryony said by way of answering for me.

I refused to cry again in front of her. She didn't need to be upset and confused. "Mommy is okay. Let's get you a bath. Go pick out your pajamas and bath toys, and I'll be right there," I told her.

She nodded and ran down the hallway.

"We talked about next year. We don't see it the same way. It ended badly," I told her. "But let me get her in bed. If I talk about it, I'll cry some more, and she doesn't need to see that."

Mom nodded. "Okay. Go take care of her. I'll be here."

She would always be there. She was my safety net. I wanted to cry thinking about how important she was to me and how making tough decisions for Bryony wasn't just my job but what I wanted to do. Because one day I wanted her to know I was her safety net. I was always there.

Brady would look back on tonight and thank me. Maybe not to my face, but he would think it. That I saved him from throwing away his youth on a girl and a kid that wasn't his. He deserved to live his life at college like he had always planned. Taking us with him was impossible not just for us but for him, too. He had practices and games and classes. We didn't fit into that.

Knowing my decision was right didn't make it any easier. Telling myself that one day it wouldn't hurt like this didn't help me. Not in this moment. In this moment I loved Brady Higgens, and life without him broke my heart into a million pieces.

The fear that I'd always love him was there. That this

pain wouldn't go away and that moving on would never really happen. Because my heart would go with Brady. He'd have it even when he no longer wanted it.

Once Bryony was bathed and asleep in bed, I went back to the living room, where Mom was still sitting, her crossword puzzle forgotten in her lap as she stared out the window in thought. She was worrying about me. Again.

"He wanted us to move to Tuscaloosa and live in family housing with him," I told her.

She sighed and patted the spot beside her. "That would never work."

"I know," I replied.

"Did you tell him your plans?"

"Yes. He didn't take it well. It ended in him yelling and telling me to leave."

"Oh, honey," she said, wrapping her arm around me and pulling me against her side. "He just loves you and doesn't want to be away from you. He'll calm down and regret it."

I had seen the look in his eyes, and I knew he wasn't going to understand and come apologize. He was hurt. I had hurt him, and after what he had gone through with his dad he wasn't going to forgive this kind of hurt easily.

And I couldn't agree to go with him just to make him happy. That wasn't the answer for either of us.

I had to keep reminding myself that one day he would see I was right.

It didn't make right now hurt any less.

The next week Bryony said Brady's name for the first time. After three days of no call or visit from him, Bryony had looked up at me with a confused expression and asked, "Bwady?"

I had no way of explaining this to her. She was too small to understand, and I'd let him into our lives. I wondered if she would ask about Coralee next. I didn't want to take her away from Coralee. She enjoyed Bryony just as much as Bryony enjoyed her. But that was an impossible situation. Especially right now.

Maybe one day it wouldn't be hard.

The doorbell rang on Thursday, and I had just checked on Grandmamma in her room. She was sorting through old books. I wasn't sure why, but that was what she was doing to occupy herself. I was afraid to ask, thinking it may confuse her when she had to answer.

Bryony ran to the door and tilted her head back to look up at the knob she couldn't reach yet. I went behind her and opened it, knowing it wouldn't be Brady. He was at school. The small hope still stirred inside me pointlessly.

Coralee stood on the other side of the door with a plate of cookies in one hand and a lemon cake in the other.

"I brought treats," she said with a smile.

"Cowee," Bryony called out in excitement at the sight of her friend and jumped up and down to make sure we both understood how happy she was about this.

"First he says Brady and now Coralee all in one day," I told her, stepping back to let her in. "She's missed you."

Coralee smiled down at Bryony. "And I've missed her. Very much."

I took the two plates from Coralee and walked them to the kitchen while Coralee bent down to scoop up Bryony. I knew this visit wasn't just about Bryony. She was here to talk about Brady. I just didn't know what her view would be.

I walked back into the living room and sat down in the recliner. "How have you been?" I asked her, since I had grown used to seeing her regularly.

She sighed. "Well, you two have been missed. Especially by the boy in my house. He's not the same."

"I miss him too," I told her.

"He explained what happened. I agree with you. That's not a life for a child. But only a parent can understand that."

If only Brady could get it. "I just hope one day he understands."

"It doesn't have to be either/or, though. You can build

your life here and he can go there. If it's meant to be, the two of you will find a way. Acting as if being apart is impossible will only hurt the two of you."

Bryony was snuggled up in Coralee's arms. The sight made me teary-eyed. "How would it work? We would see each other one weekend a month? Talk on the phone? Those relationships don't seem possible."

Coralee leaned back on the sofa to get more comfortable. "They don't work if the couple isn't meant to be. But if you love someone you can wait forever. Each moment you're together is special. You live for those times. College isn't forever."

I had no argument for that. If she was right, then we had a chance. The idea of life without Brady was too painful to focus on. I had been pushing it from my mind all week.

"He isn't going to forgive me," I told her.

She gave me a small smile. "Sweetie, he forgave you before you left the drive. But he's hurt. He thinks he wasn't enough for you. I told him this too, and he said he'd agree to anything to be with you. But he said you weren't wanting to do that. I knew he was wrong. That's why I'm here."

He wanted to try. That was enough for me. This week was enough for me to know I would do whatever I could to make this work.

CHAPTER 56

BRADY

I walked out to my truck after school with the same heaviness I had carried all damn week. It wasn't getting easier. I was growing more miserable by the day.

I'd started to open my truck door when I saw a small blue envelope tucked in my windshield wipers. Pausing, I reached over and plucked it out of the wipers' grasp. Tossing my book bag in the car, I climbed inside and opened the envelope.

> Brady,
> I miss you. Can we talk?
> Riley

She hadn't texted me. She'd come up here and left me a simple handwritten note. What did that mean? Did I still have a chance to save us? To keep her?

I picked up my phone and started to dial her number, then stopped. I wasn't sure I was strong enough to hear her voice yet. Especially if she was telling me she was leaving or some terrible shit like that.

So I texted her. "Yes, we can talk. Where?"

The text came back within seconds. "The field."

That was as secluded as we could get.

"Headed there now."

"Okay."

I started the truck and turned it toward the road. Seeing her again was all I'd thought I needed every day this week. Now that I was about to, I was scared shitless. If she was going to tell me again how we couldn't work, I wasn't sure my heart could take it.

The drive to the field was short with me speeding. My anxiety and fear were coiling inside me and I was a mess by the time I pulled up beside her red Mustang.

She wasn't in it, so I climbed out and headed for the center of the field.

I saw her brown hair blowing in the breeze as she stood among the wildflowers that grew in the field this time of year. She reminded me of a painting someone would hang on their wall. Everything about her beautiful. Inside and out. For a brief moment she had been mine. Or I had been hers.

She turned and her eyes locked with mine.

There were a million things I wanted to say, but they all fell away as I stood there looking at her. The girl who had changed my world. Been my strength when I hadn't had any and shown me that life was about the good *and* bad times.

"I can't live in Tuscaloosa. But I don't want that to be the end of us. I can wait for you. I'll follow my plan, but I'll stay here and in Nashville until you finish college. You chase your dream and I'll build mine. We don't have to choose, Brady. We can each have what is best for us and each other, too."

She sounded like she had talked to my mom.

"I was wrong to think you should pack up your life and move to Tuscaloosa with Bryony. She needs Lawton and the people in it. She's secure here. I was being selfish. I can love you just as much in Tuscaloosa as I do here. Distance isn't going to change that."

Her eyes filled with tears, and she took a step toward me. This was what I wanted. Her close to me. "I do love you. I hate that you think I don't."

I sighed and pulled her the rest of the way to me. "I didn't mean it. I was upset and scared."

She curled into me and laid her head on my chest. "I

can come to your games and during your off-season you can come here on some weekends. We can make it work. It doesn't matter where you are. I will always love you."

I pressed a kiss to her temple and closed my eyes. I would love her until the day I died. I didn't question that. She was my piece in this world. The piece that completed me.

"One day I'll ask you to marry me," I told her.

"And one day I'll say yes," she replied.

For now, that was enough.

Acknowledgments

A big thank you to my editor, Jennifer Ung. She worked with me and my crazy schedule due to being pregnant while working on this book. With her help I believe we made it the best it could be. I'm very proud of how it turned out. Also I want to mention Mara Anastas, Jodie Hockensmith, Carolyn Swerdloff, and the rest of the Simon Pulse team, for all their hard work in getting my books out there.

My agent, Jane Dystel. She's there for me when I'm having a hard time working on a story, when I need to vent, and even if I just need a recommendation on a good place to eat in New York City. I'm thankful to have her on my side.

When I started writing I never imagined having a group of readers come together for the sole purpose of supporting me. Abbi's Army, led by Danielle Lagasse and Vicci Kaighan, humbles me and gives me a place of refuge. When I need my spirits lifted, these ladies are there. I love every one of you.

Last but certainly not least: my family. Without their support I wouldn't be here. My kids who understand my deadlines and help around the house. My parents, who have supported me all along. Even when I decided to write steamier stuff. My friends, who don't hate me because I can't because my writing is taking over. They are my ultimate support group, and I love them dearly.

Britt Sullivan for listening to me rant, helping me work through storylines, and understanding how moody I can be when writing a book. He's not only a wonderful father but a man that I am thankful to have by my side.

My readers. I never expected to have so many of you. Thank you for reading my books. For loving them and telling others about them. Without you I wouldn't be here. It's that simple.